A BITE OF PEPPER

A BITE OF PEPPER

BALAZS LORINCZI

MARGARET K. McELDERRY BOOKS
NEW YORK • AMSTERDAM/ANTWERP • LONDON
TORONTO • SYDNEY/MELBOURNE • NEW DELHI

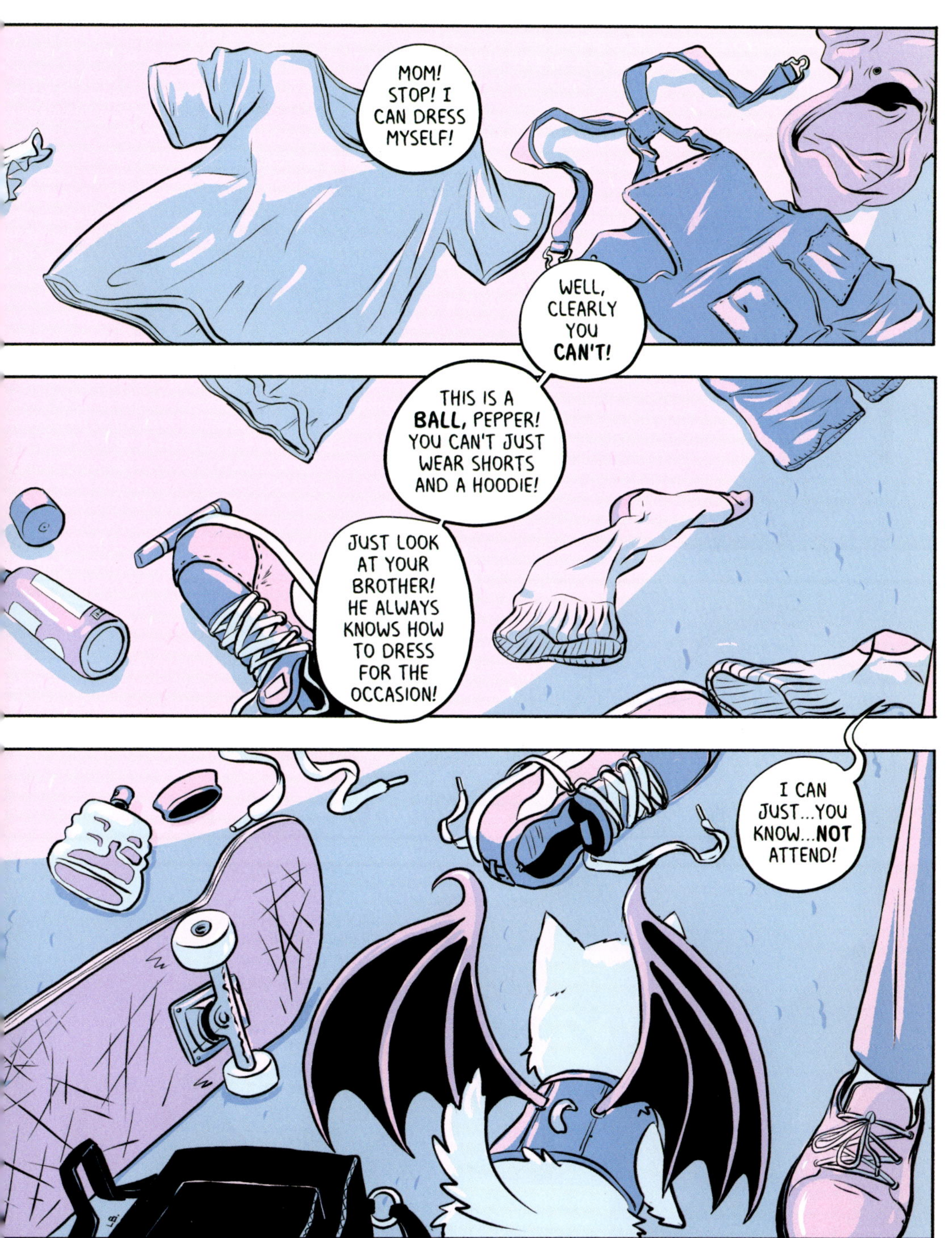
MOM! STOP! I CAN DRESS MYSELF!
WELL, CLEARLY YOU **CAN'T**!
THIS IS A **BALL**, PEPPER! YOU CAN'T JUST WEAR SHORTS AND A HOODIE!
JUST LOOK AT YOUR BROTHER! HE ALWAYS KNOWS HOW TO DRESS FOR THE OCCASION!
I CAN JUST...YOU KNOW...**NOT** ATTEND!

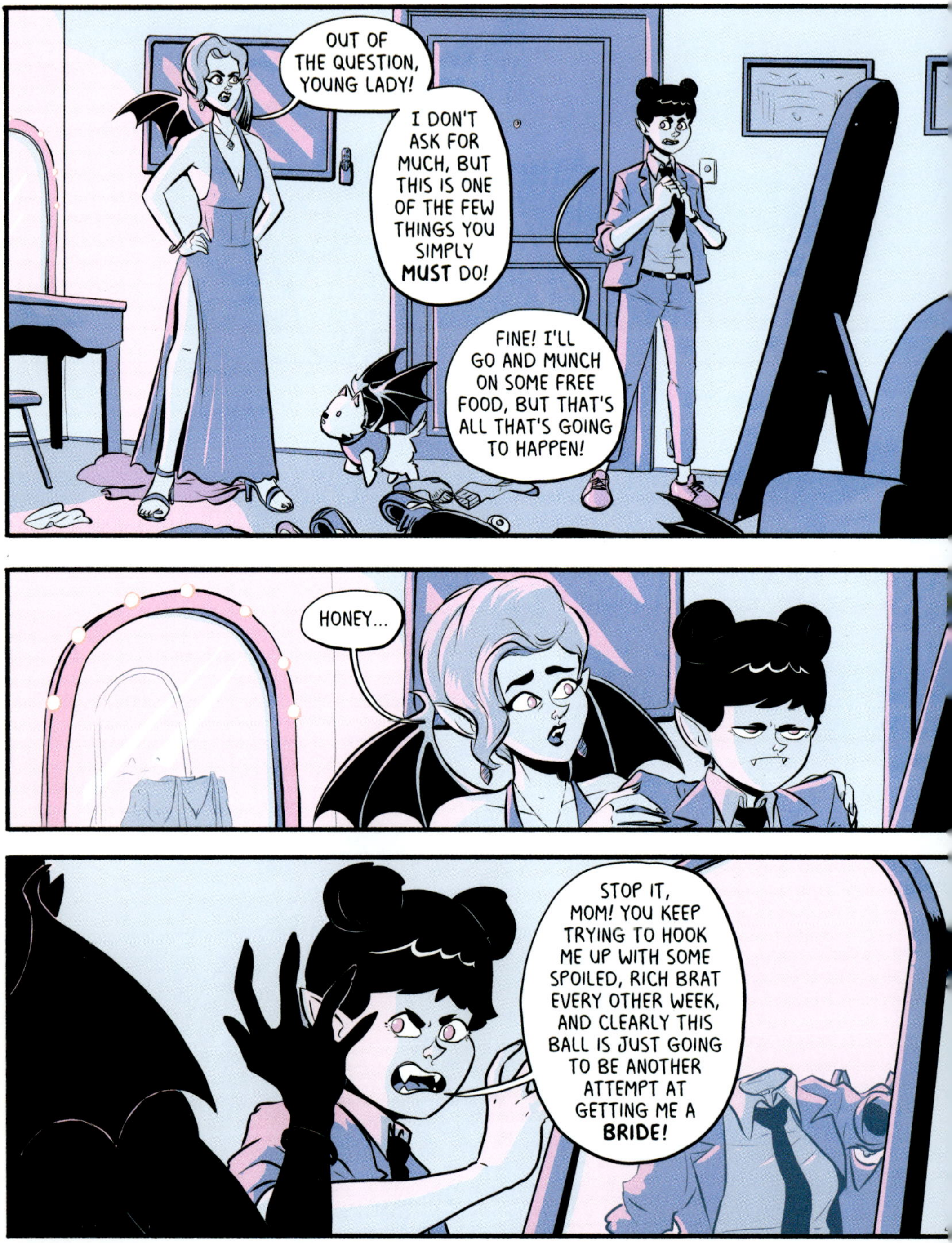

OUT OF THE QUESTION, YOUNG LADY!
I DON'T ASK FOR MUCH, BUT THIS IS ONE OF THE FEW THINGS YOU SIMPLY **MUST** DO!
FINE! I'LL GO AND MUNCH ON SOME FREE FOOD, BUT THAT'S ALL THAT'S GOING TO HAPPEN!

THE CEREMONY IS COMING UP, PEPPER, AND IF YOU DON'T FIND SOMEONE SOON, YOU WILL HAVE TO WAIT ANOTHER YEAR TO **FULLY** BECOME A VAMPIRE!

AND WHAT A TRAGEDY THAT WOULD BE!

WHAT?

YOU **KNOW** WHAT! THIS IS IMPORTANT!
YES, BECAUSE IT'S ABOUT YOUR WELL-BEING!
TO **YOU!**

SURE...

UGH! LOOK, JUST...GO OUT AND TRY TO HAVE SOME FUN, PLEASE. AND MAYBE MAKE SOME CONNECTIONS?
I CAN'T PROMISE ANY--

HEY!
SHOVE!

RESSING
ROOM 2
WHAT ABOUT SHROOM?
HE'S A GOOD BOY. HE WILL WAIT HERE FOR YOU.
MRR?

SIGH...
STOP SIGHING AND GO MINGLE!
FANGS & WINGS BALL

UMM...

SORRY!
SORRY!
COMING
THROUGH!
HEY!
WAITER!
OVER
HERE!

AH, SORRY,
MY TRAY
IS EMPTY.
I NEED TO
REFILL!
ANA!
WHERE
THE **HECK**
ARE YOU?

I...UMM...
JUST STUCK
IN THE MIDDLE
OF THE CROWD,
BOSS!

WELL, GET
BACK IN THE
KITCHEN **ASAP!**
WE HAVE A PILE
OF TRAYS HERE
THAT NEEDS TO
BE CARRIED
OUT!

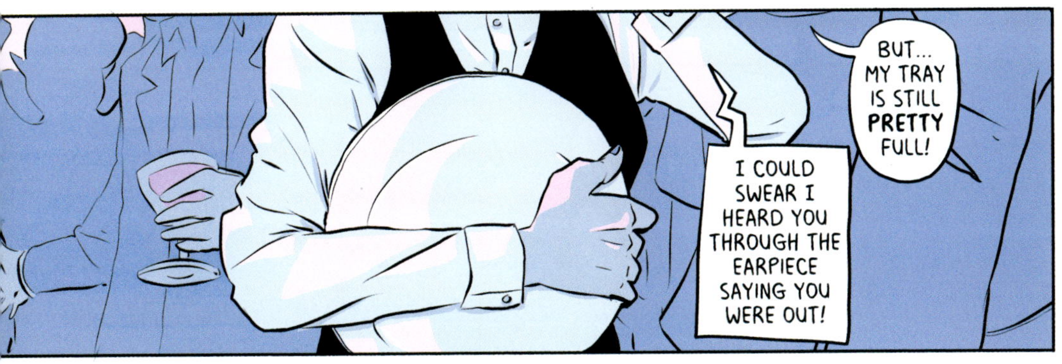
BUT...
MY TRAY
IS STILL
PRETTY
FULL!
I COULD
SWEAR I
HEARD YOU
THROUGH THE
EARPIECE
SAYING YOU
WERE OUT!

SORRY, BOSS!
YOU ARE BREAKING
UP! THE RECEPTION
GOT REALLY BAD
HERE!
TAP
TAP
TAP

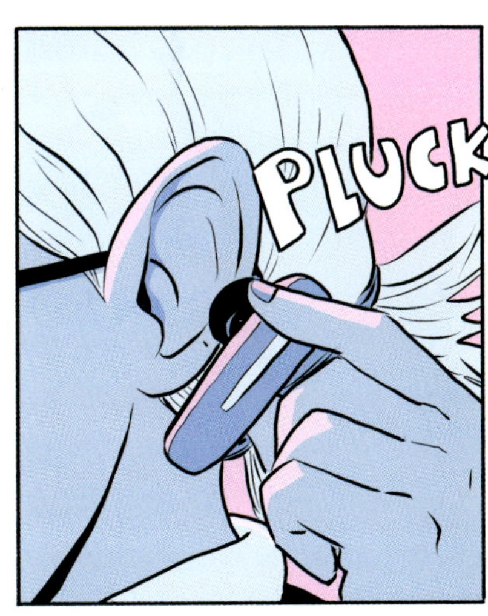
PLUCK

TIME FOR A SNEAKY BREAK!

HUFF...

AND THEN SHE JUST WENT ON AND SANG IT ANYWAY!
REGARDLESS, I ALWAYS SAID IN THE BLA BLA BLAA BLA BLA...

BLA BLA BLABLA BLA BLA BLAA BLA BLABLAB...

BLAAB BLE BLEE BLABLA BLA!

OHOHO HOHO!

ERR... HAHA, FUNNY STORY OR WHATEVER. OH, LOOK I'M OUT OF B+ JUICE!

I'LL BE BACK IN A JIFFY!

HUFF!
LOOK, I JUST WANTED TO CHAT!
AND I JUST WANTED A MOMENT FOR MYSELF!
AT LEAST TELL ME YOUR NAME? I TOLD YOU MINE!

I DIDN'T ASK FOR IT THOUGH.

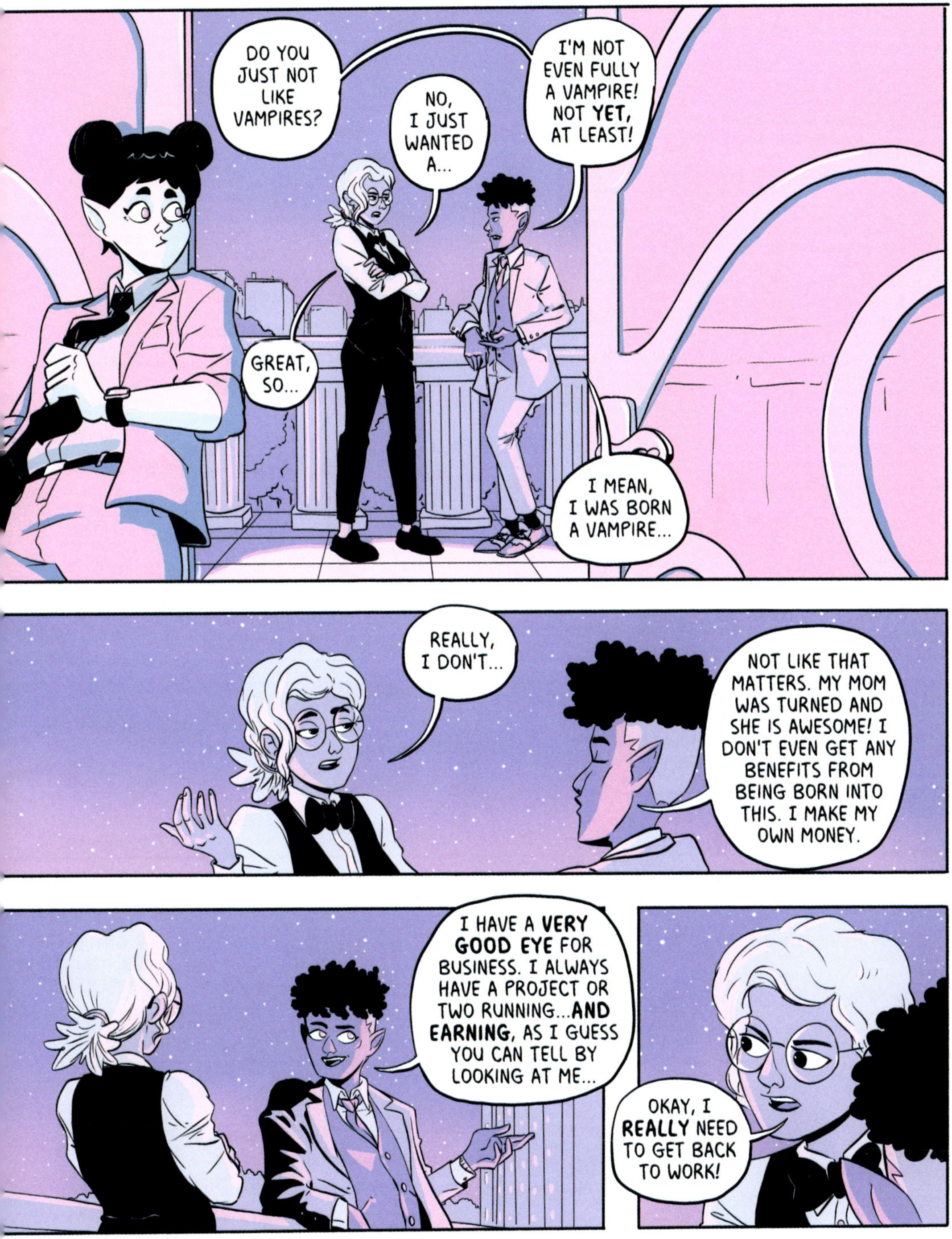

DO YOU JUST NOT LIKE VAMPIRES?
I'M NOT EVEN FULLY A VAMPIRE! NOT **YET**, AT LEAST!
NO, I JUST WANTED A...
GREAT, SO...
I MEAN, I WAS BORN A VAMPIRE...

WAIT!

DO YOU REALLY, THOUGH?

UMM...

HOW ABOUT WE JUST--

Poke!
AGH!
STOP THAT RIGHT THERE, JEB, YOU LITTLE MISCREANT!
LB.

WHAT THE HECK, PEPPER! YOU WANT TO **BLIND ME?**

YOU TRIED TO **HYPNOTIZE** HER, YOU LITTLE SLEAZEBAG!
YOU KNOW I **CAN'T** DO THAT YET!
DIDN'T STOP YOU FROM TRYING!

UMM, FOR THE RECORD, I DON'T THINK I WAS HYPNOTIZED. I WAS JUST KINDA BAFFLED.

OKAY, OKAY! MESSAGE RECEIVED! I'M GONNA BE WASHING MY EYES OUT IF ANYONE NEEDS ME.

WHICH IS NO ONE!

ERR...
OH! SORRY! HOW RUDE OF ME!

HI! I'M ANA.

THANKS FOR THE SAVE!

PEP...

PEP?
PEPPER! I'M PEPPER! **PEPPER MINT!**

OH WOW, THAT'S A COOL NA--

WAIT! ARE YOU RELATED TO **SPEAR MINT?** FROM THE TV ADS?
UGH, I DIDN'T THINK ANYONE WATCHED TV ANYMORE. IT'S SO EMBARRASSING.
BUT YEAH, SHE IS MY MOM.

I SOMETIMES PUT THE TV ON AS BACKGROUND NOISE WHEN I'M WORKING ON SOMETHING LATE AT NIGHT. AND I KEEP HEARING HER AD OVER AND OVER.
SHE MUST HAVE BOUGHT A BIG CHUNK OF LATE-NIGHT AD SPACE, HAHA!
YEAH, YOU GET A DISCOUNT ON THOSE.
ADVERTISING AN ANTIQUES SHOP TO NIGHT OWLS **AND** SAVING MONEY. IT KINDA MAKES SENSE, NOW THAT I'M THINKING ABOUT IT.

YEAH...
UMM...

SO,
WHAT ARE
YOU DOING
HERE...?

I MEAN,
UH, YOU ARE
WORKING,
OBVIOUSLY!
DUH!

SORRY, I'M NOT GREAT WITH THESE SOCIAL EVENTS, AND MY BRAIN IS KINDA MALFUNCTIONING A BIT RIGHT NOW BECAUSE OF ALL THE NOISE AND PEOPLE.
HEY, DON'T WORRY, I GET IT! WHY DO YOU THINK **I'M** OUT HERE AND NOT SERVING DRINKS INSIDE?

TOO MANY VAMPIRES?

TOO MANY **ANYONE**! I ALWAYS THINK I CAN HANDLE BEING IN A CROWD. THEN I FIND MYSELF RUNNING AWAY, HIDING ON A BALCONY, BEING HIT ON BY SOME WEIRDO.

YEAH, SORRY ABOUT THAT. THAT WEIRDO IS ACTUALLY MY HALF BROTHER. HE'S NOT A BAD KID, HE'S JUST...A BIT MUCH.
HE'S VERY EAGER TO GET AHEAD OF ME WITH HIS **TURNING.**
I WILL JUST NOD AND PRETEND I KNOW WHAT YOU ARE TALKING ABOUT, SO I WON'T EMBARRASS MYSELF.
YOU DON'T KNOW WHAT THE TURNING IS?
NOT A CLUE.
OH... I JUST THOUGHT WORKING AT A **VAMPIRE** EVENT, YOU MUST BE...
A FANGIRL?
KINDA?

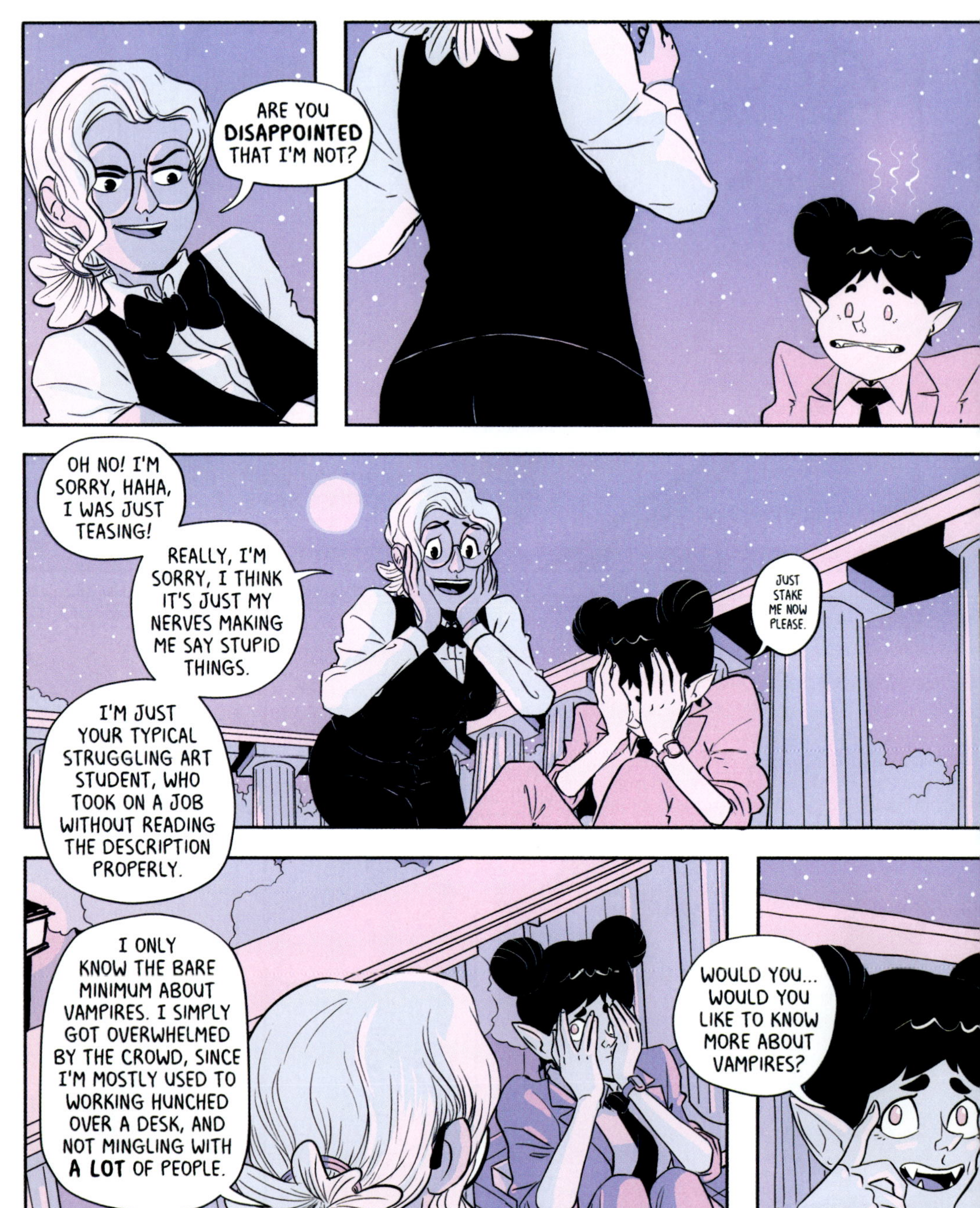
ARE YOU **DISAPPOINTED** THAT I'M NOT?
OH NO! I'M SORRY, HAHA, I WAS JUST TEASING!
REALLY, I'M SORRY, I THINK IT'S JUST MY NERVES MAKING ME SAY STUPID THINGS.
I'M JUST YOUR TYPICAL STRUGGLING ART STUDENT, WHO TOOK ON A JOB WITHOUT READING THE DESCRIPTION PROPERLY.
JUST STAKE ME NOW PLEASE.
I ONLY KNOW THE BARE MINIMUM ABOUT VAMPIRES. I SIMPLY GOT OVERWHELMED BY THE CROWD, SINCE I'M MOSTLY USED TO WORKING HUNCHED OVER A DESK, AND NOT MINGLING WITH **A LOT** OF PEOPLE.
WOULD YOU... WOULD YOU LIKE TO KNOW MORE ABOUT VAMPIRES?

YOU KNOW WHAT? I WOULD LO--

ANA! ANA WHERE THE **HECK** ARE YOU?

OH NO! THAT'S MY BOSS!
I GOT ONE OF THE GUESTS COMPLAINING ABOUT YOU!

JEB!

I'M **SO** FIRED.
NOW MOM WON'T LEAVE ME ALONE ALL NIGHT.

ARE YOU THINKING WHAT **I'M** THINKING?
IS MIND READING SOMETHING VAMPIRES CAN DO?
SOME OF THEM, YES, BUT NOT UNTIL MY TURNING, AND EVEN THEN I DON'T THINK THAT'S GONNA BE MY--

ACTUALLY, THIS GAVE ME AN IDEA.
WHAT IF, INSTEAD OF GETTING CHEWED OUT BY YOUR BOSS AND MY MOM, WE SKIP THIS PARTY AND I EXPLAIN EVERYTHING ABOUT VAMPIRES THAT YOU NEVER WANTED TO KNOW? SOMEWHERE ELSE, LESS BUSY.

SOUNDS PRETTY IDEAL, TO BE HONEST. BUT HOW ARE WE GOING TO SNEAK PAST THEM? THEY ARE ABOUT TO STORM UP HERE ANY SECOND NOW!

THAT'S WHERE **SHROOM** COMES INTO THE PICTURE!

WHO?

INHALE

SHROOM!
BACKPACK!

WHAT THE HECK WAS THAT?

KH-RASH!

AND WHAT THE HECK WAS **THAT**?
THAT, MY FRIEND...

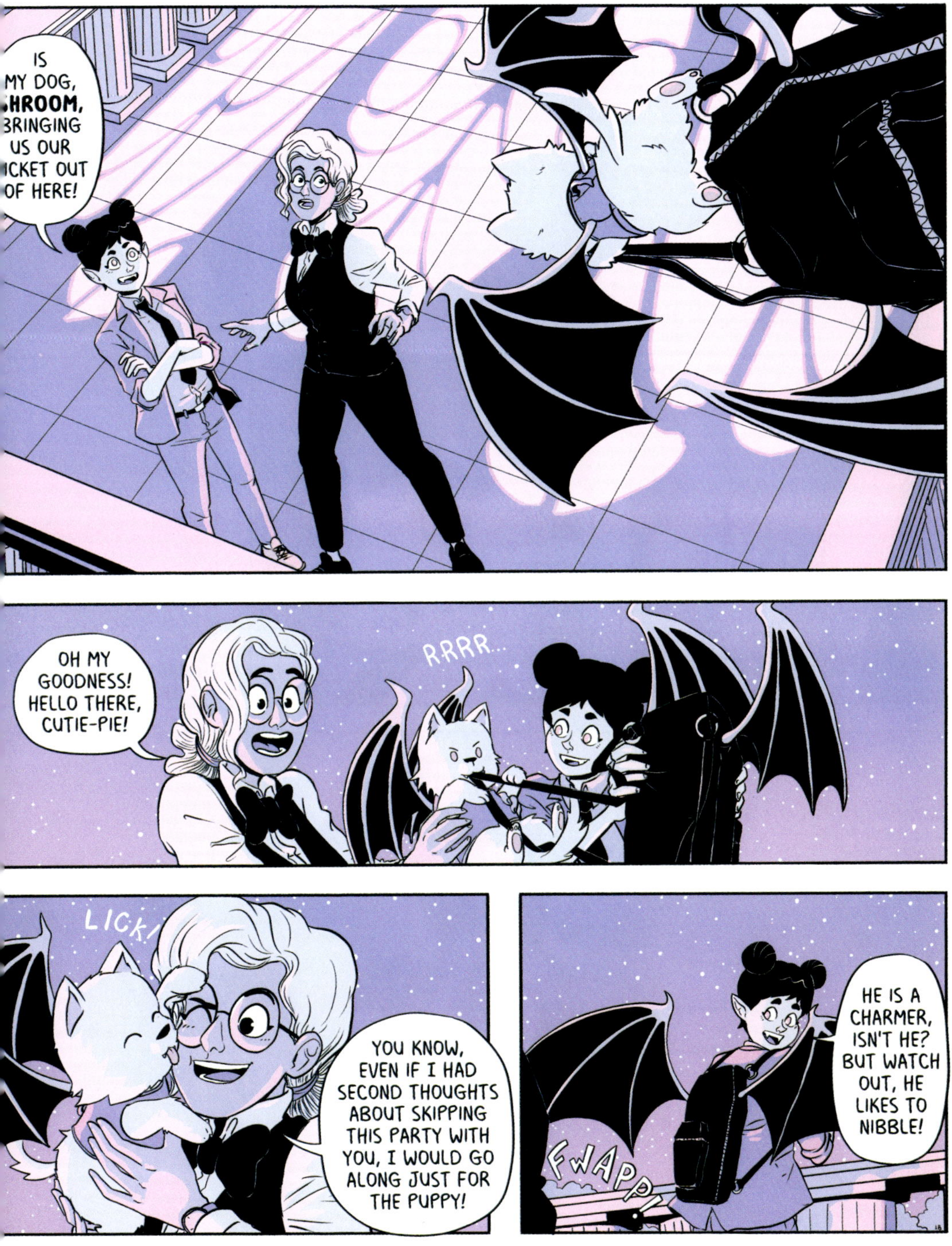

IS
MY DOG,
HROOM,
BRINGING
US OUR
ICKET OUT
OF HERE!

ALL RIGHT, M'LADY! HOLD ON TO YOUR SPECS!
WAIT! ARE YOU PLANNING TO...**FLY** US OUT OF HERE? WITH YOUR **BACKPACK?**

WELL, KINDA...
PEPPER!

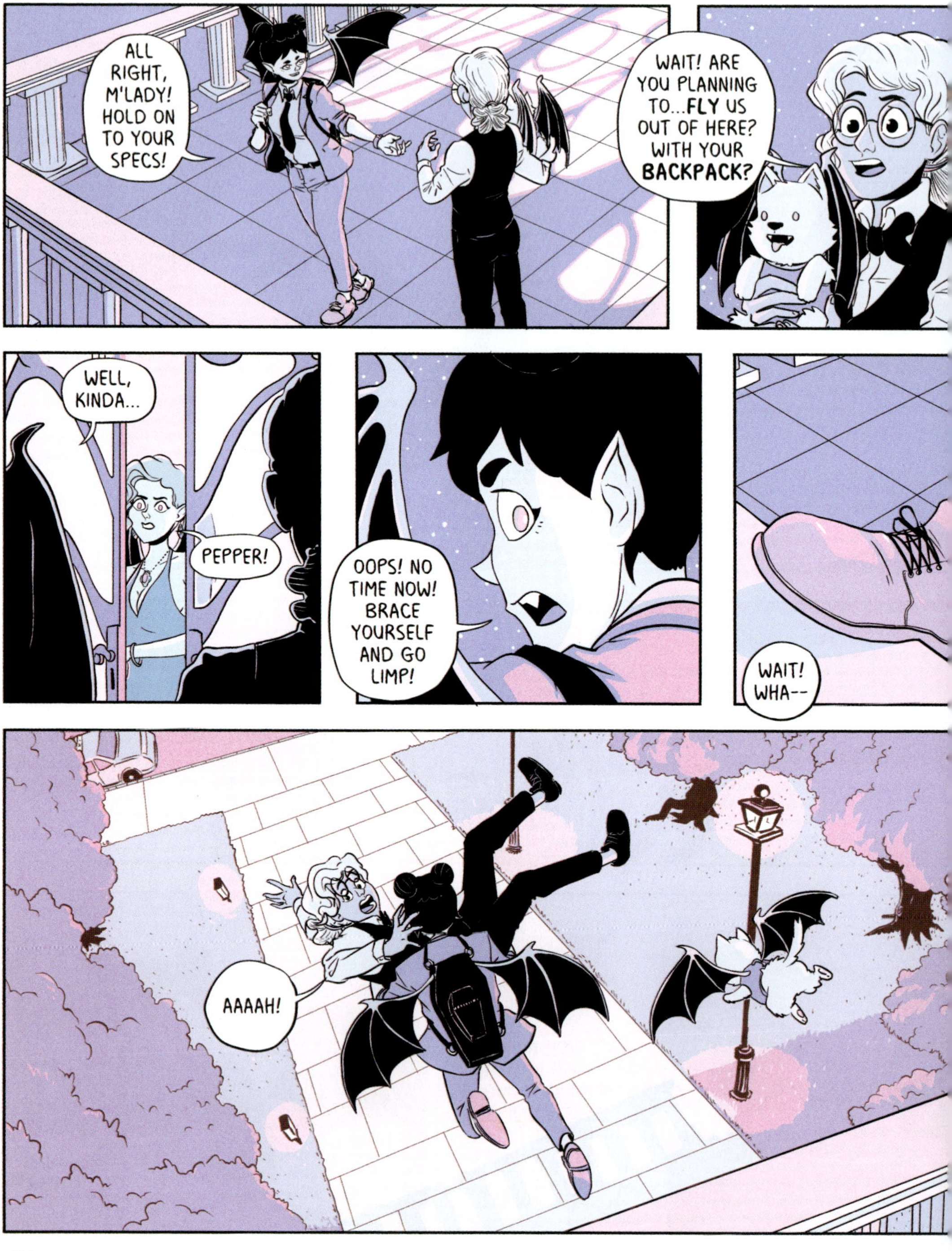

OOPS! NO TIME NOW! BRACE YOURSELF AND GO LIMP!

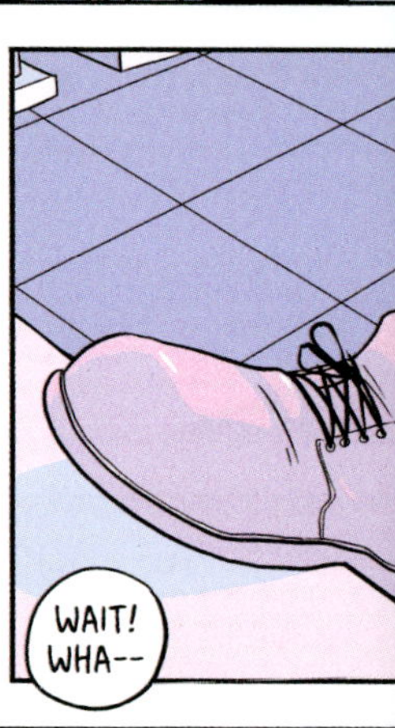
WAIT! WHA--

AAAAH!

BACK ENTRY

STOP FIDGETING, YOU'LL FALL!
BACK ENTRY

BACK ENTRY

OW!

ANA!
BACK ENTRY
OH NO! PEPPER! I THINK I KILLED SOMEONE!

HE'S A VAMPIRE. HE'S GONNA BE FINE... EVENTUALLY.

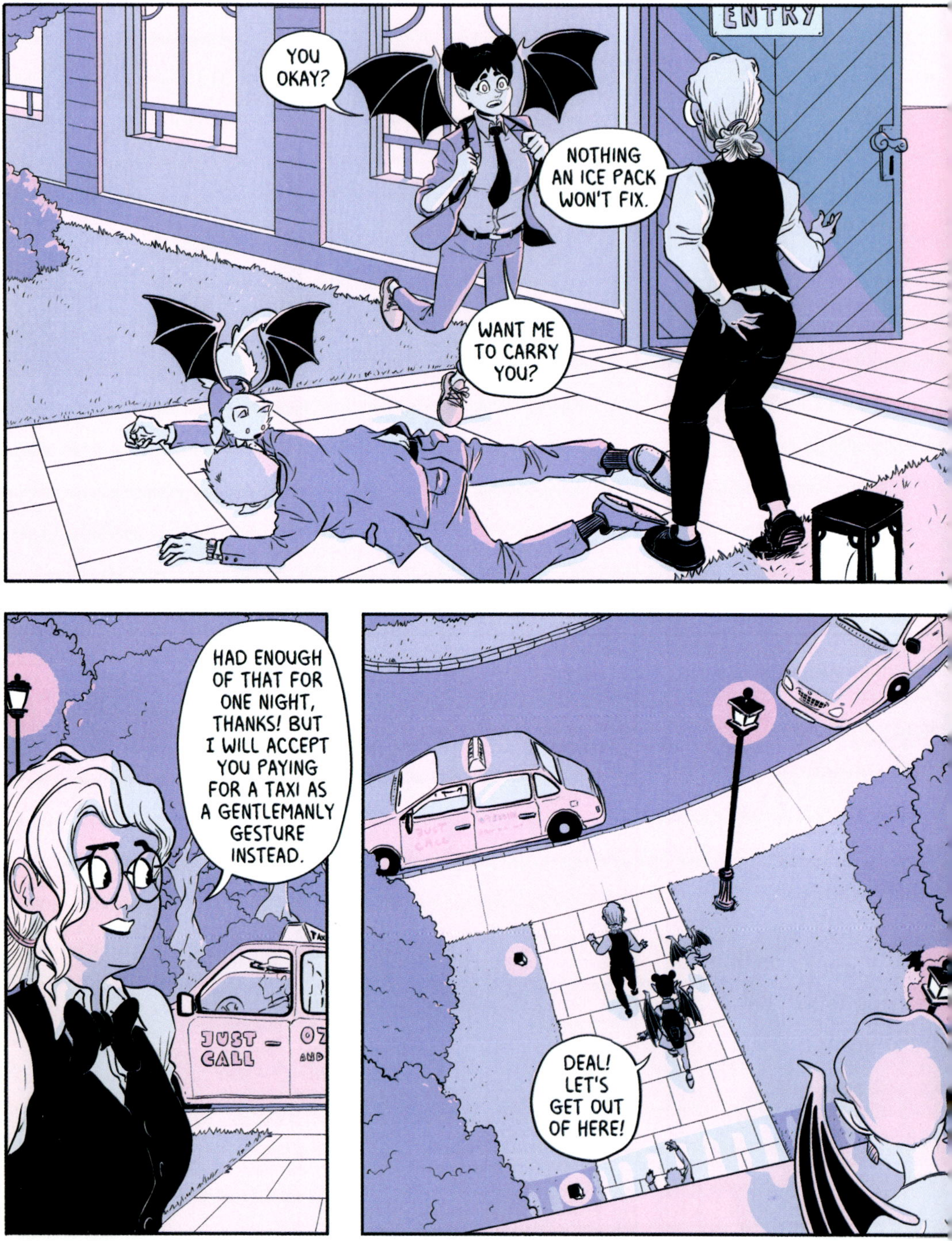

ENTRY
YOU OKAY?
NOTHING AN ICE PACK WON'T FIX.
WANT ME TO CARRY YOU?

WHERE ARE WE GOING?

I HAVE AN IDEA...

OOOH!
THAT'S MY SPECIALTY!
I CAN TELL!

OKAY, WAIT!

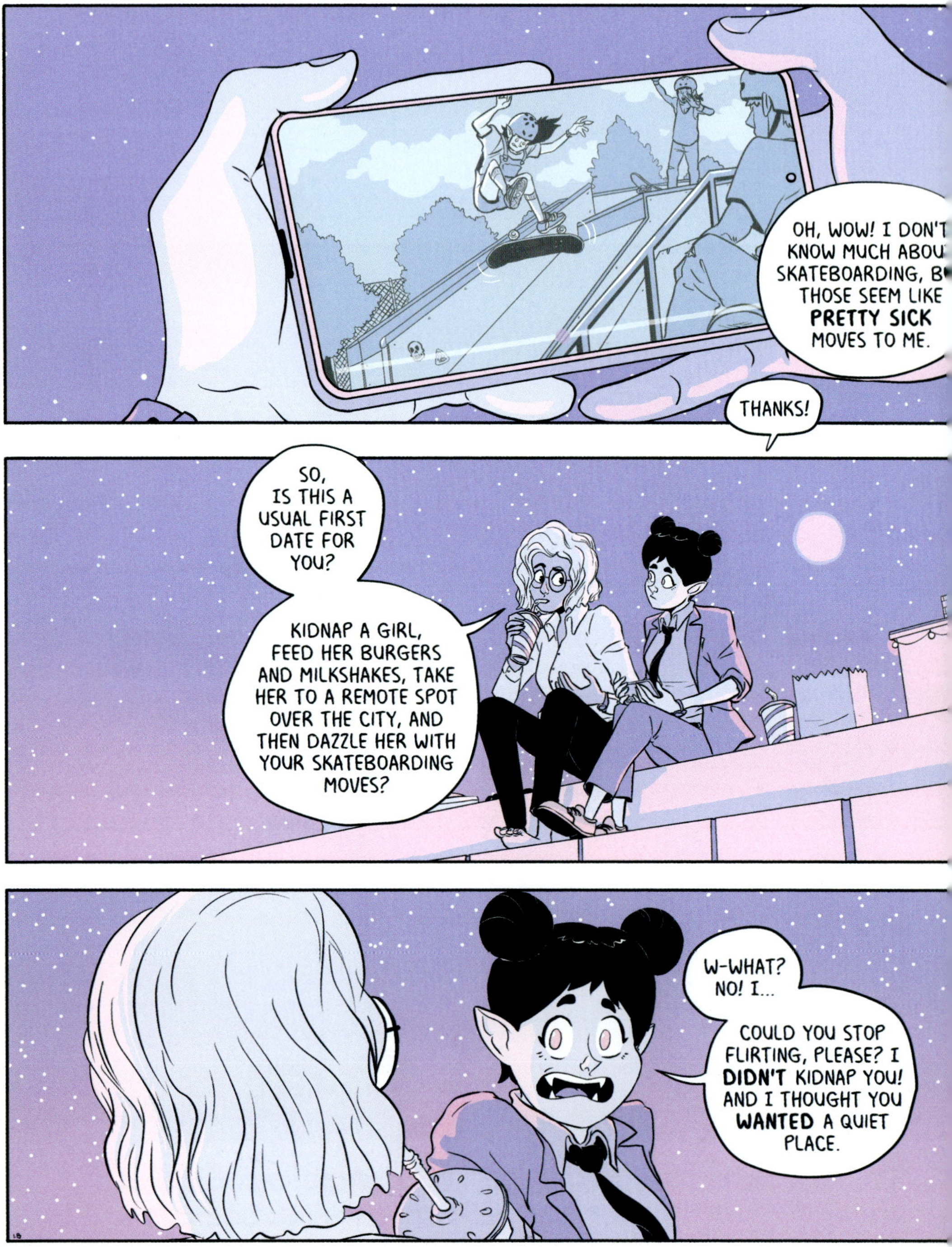

OH, WOW! I DON'T KNOW MUCH ABOU SKATEBOARDING, B THOSE SEEM LIKE **PRETTY SICK** MOVES TO ME.

THANKS!

SO, IS THIS A USUAL FIRST DATE FOR YOU?

KIDNAP A GIRL, FEED HER BURGERS AND MILKSHAKES, TAKE HER TO A REMOTE SPOT OVER THE CITY, AND THEN DAZZLE HER WITH YOUR SKATEBOARDING MOVES?

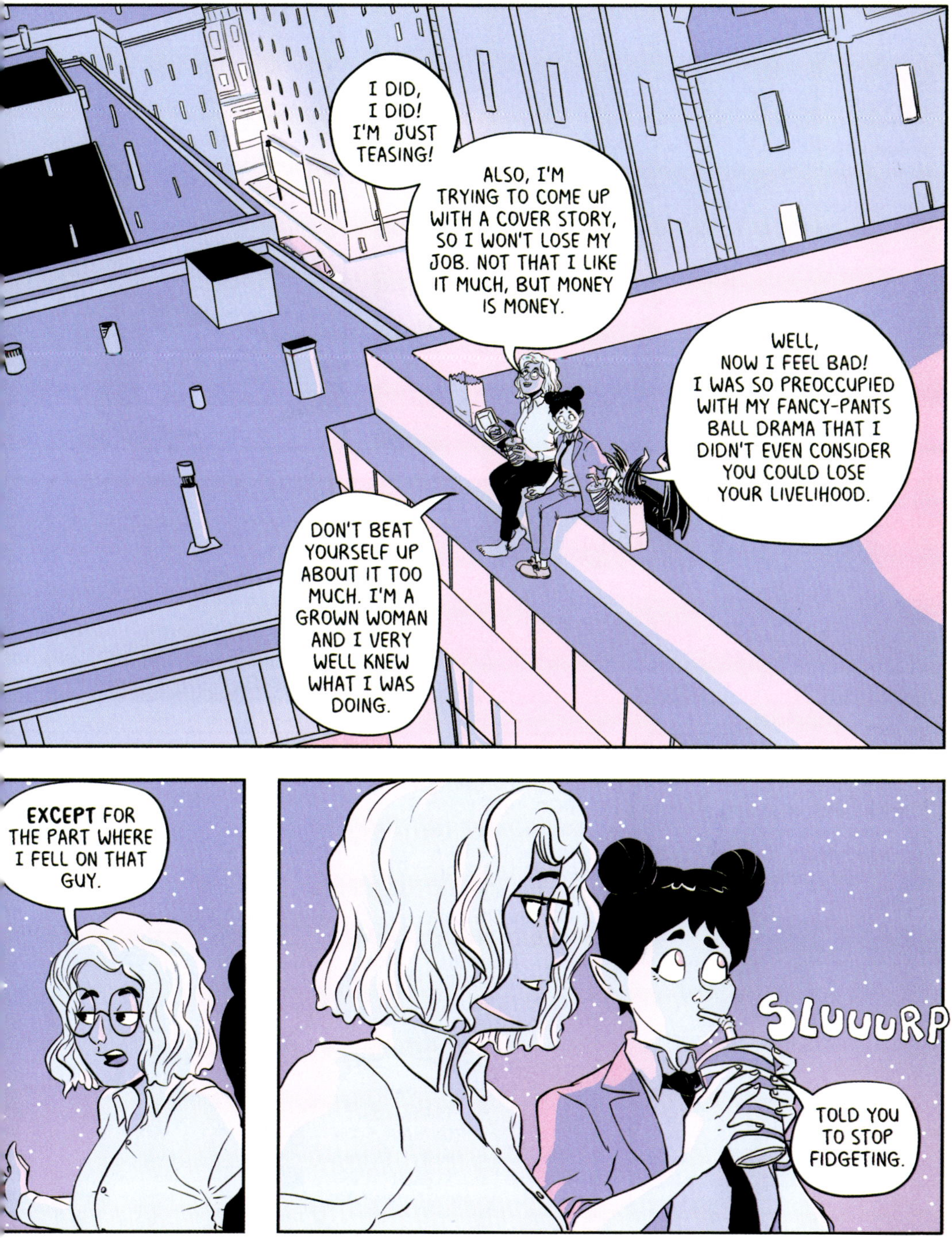

I DID, I DID! I'M JUST TEASING!

ALSO, I'M TRYING TO COME UP WITH A COVER STORY, SO I WON'T LOSE MY JOB. NOT THAT I LIKE IT MUCH, BUT MONEY IS MONEY.

WELL, NOW I FEEL BAD! I WAS SO PREOCCUPIED WITH MY FANCY-PANTS BALL DRAMA THAT I DIDN'T EVEN CONSIDER YOU COULD LOSE YOUR LIVELIHOOD.

DON'T BEAT YOURSELF UP ABOUT IT TOO MUCH. I'M A GROWN WOMAN AND I VERY WELL KNEW WHAT I WAS DOING.

I SURVIVED. AND I WILL SURVIVE WITHOUT A JOB FOR A BIT TOO.
MY STUDENT LOAN COVERS A HEALTHY SUPPLY OF POT NOODLES. OR YOU CAN JUST TREAT ME TO BURGERS AND SHAKES SOME OTHER TIME AS WELL.

YEAH...NOT SURE IF THAT'S A GOOD IDEA.

OH, ARE YOU THE BITE AND DUMP TYPE?

I REALLY WANT TO BE ANNOYED ABOUT YOUR VAMPIRE JOKES, BUT EVEN MORE ANNOYINGLY, THEY ARE FUNNY.

WELL, YOU CAN'T DENY THAT YOU CONVINCED ME TO FOLLOW YOU TO A SECOND LOCATION, AND THE BURGER, THAT YOU SNEAKILY TRIED TO ORDER AS **EXTRA RARE** SURELY WON'T SATIATE YOUR BLOODLUST.
HAH! BLOODLUST? YOU HAVE SOME PRETTY ROUGH STEREOTYPES ABOUT VAMPIRES.

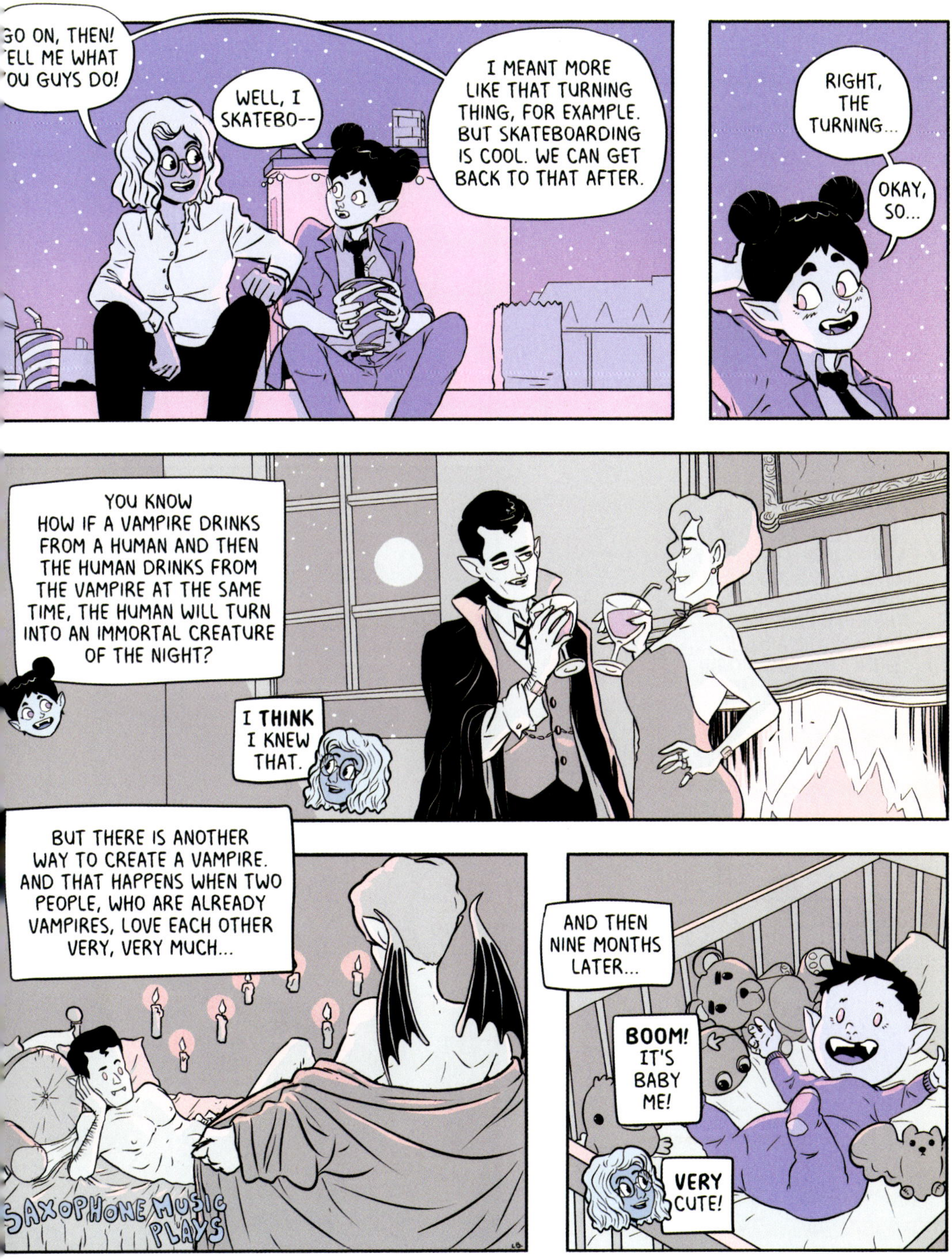

YOU KNOW HOW IF A VAMPIRE DRINKS FROM A HUMAN AND THEN THE HUMAN DRINKS FROM THE VAMPIRE AT THE SAME TIME, THE HUMAN WILL TURN INTO AN IMMORTAL CREATURE OF THE NIGHT?

I **THINK** I KNEW THAT.

BUT THERE IS ANOTHER WAY TO CREATE A VAMPIRE. AND THAT HAPPENS WHEN TWO PEOPLE, WHO ARE ALREADY VAMPIRES, LOVE EACH OTHER VERY, VERY MUCH...

SAXOPHONE MUSIC PLAYS

AND THEN NINE MONTHS LATER...

BOOM! IT'S BABY ME!

VERY CUTE!

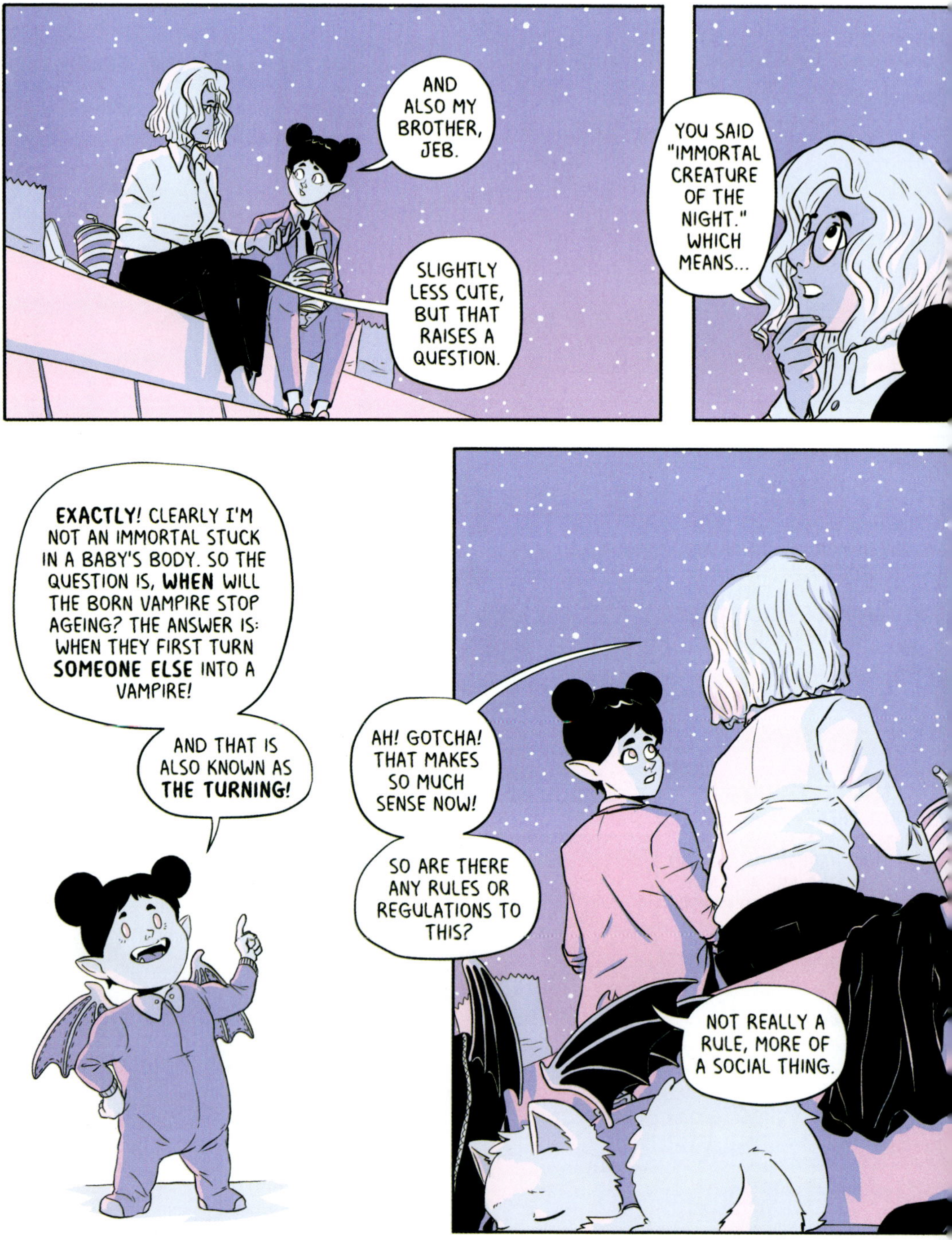

EXACTLY! CLEARLY I'M NOT AN IMMORTAL STUCK IN A BABY'S BODY. SO THE QUESTION IS, **WHEN** WILL THE BORN VAMPIRE STOP AGEING? THE ANSWER IS: WHEN THEY FIRST TURN **SOMEONE ELSE** INTO A VAMPIRE!

AND THAT IS ALSO KNOWN AS **THE TURNING!**

AH! GOTCHA! THAT MAKES SO MUCH SENSE NOW!

SO ARE THERE ANY RULES OR REGULATIONS TO THIS?

NOT REALLY A RULE, MORE OF A SOCIAL THING.

WE HAVE A FEW ANNUAL EVENTS: THE MASQUERADE, THE FESTIVAL, THE BALL WE'VE JUST BEEN TO, AND THE BIGGEST ONE, **THE GALA.**
IT'S COMMON PRACTICE FOR THE NEW COUPLES--VAMPIRES AND THEIR SOON-TO-BE-TURNED CHOSEN--TO GET ANNOUNCED THERE.
VAMPIRES HAVE ALWAYS HAD A FRAGILE RELATIONSHIP WITH HUMANS, SO WE KEEP ALL OUR EVENTS VERY VISIBLE, AND TRY TO LIMIT OUR TURNINGS TO A ONCE-A-YEAR THING, SO HUMANS WON'T FREAK OUT THAT WE ARE SECRETLY TRYING TO MULTIPLY AND TAKE OVER THE WORLD.
UNLESS YOU BELIEVE WHAT YOU READ ON... **CERTAIN PARTS** OF THE INTERNET.
AND I GUESS IT'S TIME FOR YOU AND JEB TO SCORE A... PARTNER? TURNEE?
BRIDE. REGARDLESS OF GENDER, THEY ARE CALLED BRIDES.
COOL!

5:49
yaboi_jeb
yaboi_jeb fam!
View all 35 comments
17 March
IT IS TRADITIONAL TO GET YOUR KIDS TURNED IN ORDER OF THEIR AGE. AND I'M ALMOST A YEAR OLDER THAN JEB. BUT THAT WON'T STOP HIM FROM DOING IT FIRST IF HE CAN, JUST TO PLEASE MOM.
HE'S ALWAYS BEEN A MOMMA'S BOY

I HAVE A FEELING THAT YOU ARE NOT AS ENTHUSIASTIC AS YOUR MOM AND YOUR BROTHER.

MY MOM...SHE JUST WANTS THE BEST FOR ME, REALLY. OR WHAT SHE **THINKS** IS THE BEST FOR ME.
SCROLL SCROLL

books
SPEAR MINT CONDITION
USED & ...IQUE ...OKS
MY BIOLOGICAL DAD TURNED MY MOM AS A LAST RESORT, SO HE WOULDN'T LOSE HIS INHERITANCE. HE PAID MY MOM OFF AND HASN'T BEEN SEEN SINCE.
MOM USED THE MONEY TO START A NEW LIFE, AND OPENED THE USED BOOK SHOP, BUT STRUGGLED TO FIND ANOTHER PARTNER FOR YEARS.

THEN SHE MET JEB'S DAD, THEY GOT MARRIED, AND THEN THE POOR GUY HAD A WEIRD ACCIDENT AND PASSED AWAY, LEAVING MOM WITH JEB AND ME.

AFTER THAT, SHE GOT IT INTO HER HEAD THAT SHE WAS TOO OLD WHEN SHE WAS TURNED, AND NOW SHE SPLITS HER ATTENTION BETWEEN THE SHOP AND SETTING ME UP FOR LIFE.

SHE WANTS ME TO FIND A BRIDE FOR THIS YEAR'S GALA, SO I WON'T "WASTE ANOTHER YEAR."

BUT YOU DON'T WANT IT? EVEN THOUGH IT ACTUALLY SOUNDS PRETTY NEAT TO ME, TO BECOME MMORTAL WHILE YOU ARE STILL YOUNG AND SPRY.

I KINDA WISH I HAD THE CHANCE TO NOT BE WORRIED ABOUT TIME. TO NOT CRAM MY STUDIES INTO MY YOUTH WHILE ALSO TRYING TO FUND THOSE STUDIES. BECAUSE YOU ONLY HAVE A SHORT WINDOW IN YOUR LIFE, AND AFTER THAT YOU ARE...

LOOK, I'M NOT EVEN GOING TO PRETEND I KNO HOW IT IS FOR YO TO COPE DAY-TO-D BUT I STILL KNO HOW IT FEELS TO BE...SOMEWHA HUMAN.

WHEN YOU ARE GROWING UP AND BECOMING YOUR OWN PERSON, IT'S LIKE...
LIKE A PLANT OR... OR A FLOWER, GROWING FROM A SEED, THEN BLOSSOMING.

PROPER IMMORTAL VAMPIRES DON'T GROW. THEY ARE FROZEN IN TIME...

CRYSTALLIZED.

YEAH, I THINK THAT'S THE BEST WAY TO DESCRIBE IT. VAMPIRES ARE LIKE SHINING CRYSTALS.
AGELESS AND BEAUTIFUL. BUT THERE IS NO CHANGE IN THEIR NATURE. A CRYSTAL IS A CRYSTAL FROM TOP TO BOTTOM. NO FLOWERS, LEAVES, SEEDS, ANYTHING.

IMMORTAL CREATURES ARE RIGID IN THEIR OWN, PRE-BUILT STRUCTURES. AND AS BEAUTIFUL AND VALUABLE AS THAT IS, I DON'T FEEL READY TO TAKE THAT STEP.

I DON'T FEEL LIKE THE PERSON I AM **NOW** SHOULD BE CRYSTALLIZED JUST YET.

?
ALSO I DON'T WANT TO GIVE UP SKATEBOARDING.

SKATEBOARDING? WHAT DO YOU MEAN?

I'M PRETTY AGILE AND STRONG RIGHT NOW, BUT YOU KNOW HOW STRONG A VAMPIRE IS? MOST OF THE MYTHS AND MOVIES ARE ACCURATE IN THAT REGARD.
AFTER **FULLY** BECOMING A VAMPIRE, ALL MY ACQUIRED SKATEBOARDING SKILLS BECOME IRRELEVANT. DOING A KICKFLIP OFF OF A ROOF BECOMES SO EASY IT'S NOT EXCITING OR REMARKABLE ANYMORE.

OH...I SEE! I NEVER THOUGHT ABOUT THAT. THAT'S A VERY... **UNIQUE** PROBLEM.

SORRY, I'M NOT TRYING TO BE FUNNY, JUST TRYING TO WRAP MY HEAD AROUND IT.

DOES YOUR MOM KNOW HOW YOU FEEL?
I TRIED TO TELL HER, BUT...WE ARE SO DIFFERENT. IT'S REALLY HARD FOR US TO COMMUNICATE WITHOUT BEING AT EACH OTHER'S THROATS. **YOU KNOW** HOW IT IS WITH PARENTS.
NOT REALLY. MINE WERE KIND OF... ABSENT.
OH...WELL, I FEEL SILLY NOW.
AW, NO, IT'S BEEN LIKE THIS ALL MY LIFE. IT'S NOT A COMPETITION OF WHO'S MORE MISERABLE. YOUR PROBLEMS ARE JUST AS VALID AS MINE.
SKRITCH SKRITCH SKRITCH
YEAH, BUT STILL...I KEEP BLABBERING ABOUT MY LIFE AND I KNOW BASICALLY **NOTHING** ABOUT YOURS.
EH, NOT MUCH TO KNOW, COMPARED TO A SOON-TO-BE IMMORTAL SKATEBOARDING VAMPIRE WHO KIDNAPS GIRLS FROM SOCIAL EVENTS.
PLOP!
STOP! IF I WANTED TO HIT ON YOU, I **WOULD'VE** ASKED YOU FOR **A DANCE** AT THE BALL.

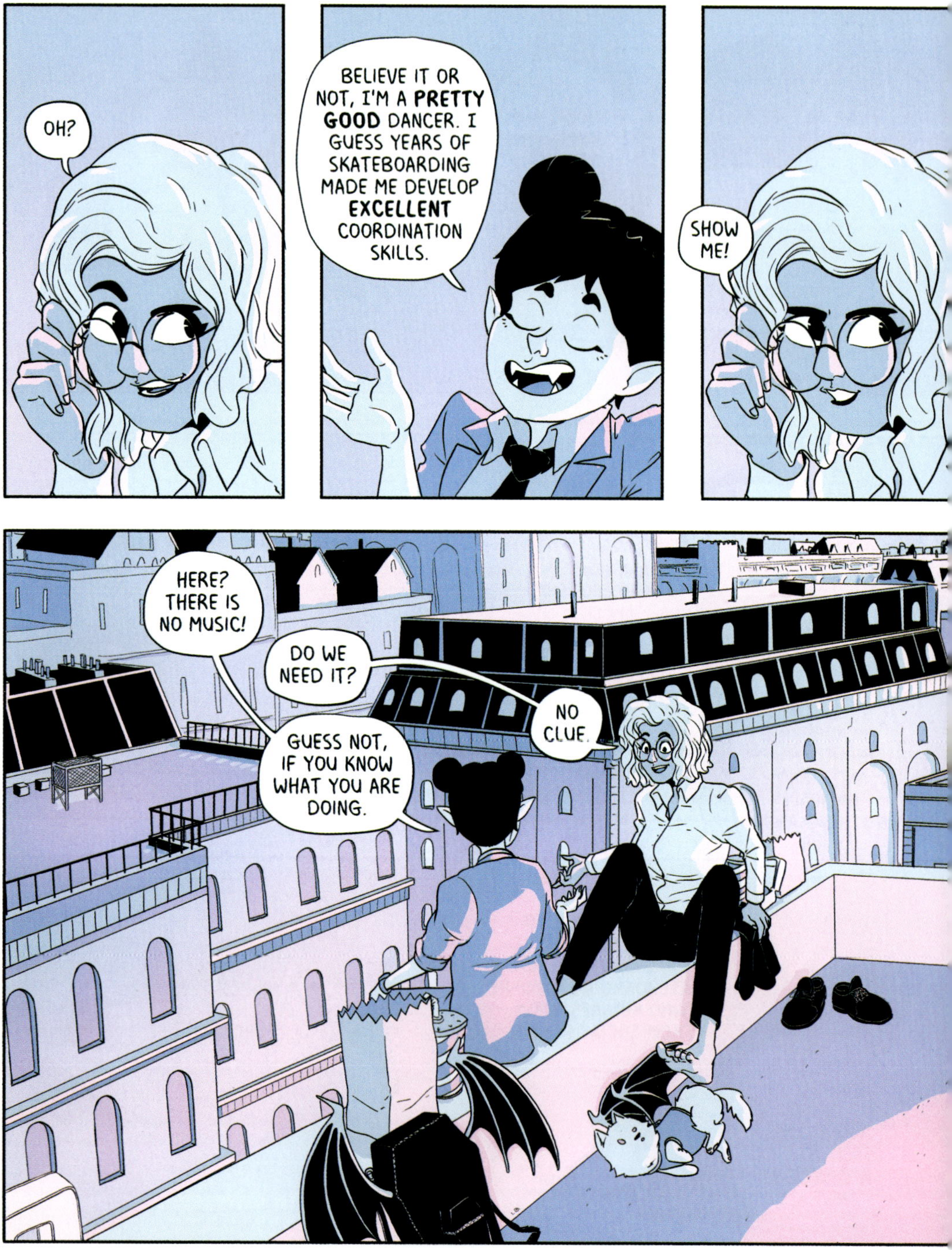

HERE? THERE IS NO MUSIC!

DO WE NEED IT?

NO CLUE.

GUESS NOT, IF YOU KNOW WHAT YOU ARE DOING.

THOUGHT SO!

OKAY, LET ME SEE...
YOU ARE TALLER, SO YOU SHOULD BE LEADING, BUT THAT WON'T BE HAPPENING, SO...

HOLD MY HAND LIKE THIS.

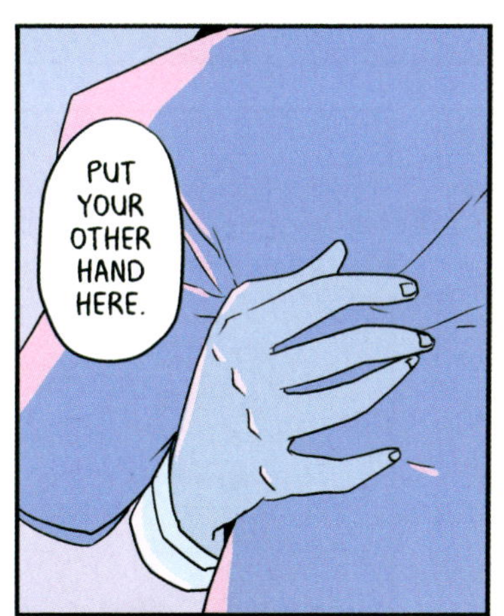
PUT YOUR OTHER HAND HERE.

PUSH THAT FOOT BACK.

THEN...

THEN...

PLOP!
PEPPER! YOU OKAY?
YEAH, JUST...
OH...
THE SUN...IS UP...

WAIT! WHAT? **THE SUN?**
ARE YOU GONNA **CATCH ON FIRE?**
PEPPER? **PEPPER!** DON'T BURST INTO FLAMES ON ME PLEASE!
SWEET, MERCIFUL DARK LORD OF THE ABYSS! **I CAN'T LET HER DIE!**
HOLD ON, PEPPER! I'LL GET YOU OUT OF THE SUN!

HOLD UP!

YOU ARE FINE!
IN FACT, VERY MUCH **NOT** BOTHERED AT ALL.

AND PEPPER ISN'T ON FIRE EITHER, WHICH MEANS...

ZZZZ

SHE JUST
FELL ASLEEP,
DIDN'T SHE?
ZZZZ

HUFF!
HUFF!
HUFF!

OKAY, OKAY, SLOW DOWN. I'M COMING!

MINT CONDITION
USED & ANTIQUE BOOKS
FINALLY! I WAS ABOUT TO COLLAPSE!

NOW WE JUST HAVE TO FIGUR OUT A WAY TO SMUGGLE YOU WITHOUT BEING NOTICED BY ANYONE.

JUST GO TO THE BACK DOOR. NO ONE EVER GOES BACK THERE AT THIS TIME.

Z Z Z Z

YES, M'LADY! MAY I **ESCORT YOU** AROUND THE BUILDING?

IT'S NOT LIKE I ALREADY DRAGGED YOUR ROYAL HIGHNESS AROUND **HALF THE CITY** OR ANYTHING!

YIP! YIP!
SHROOM! **QUIET!** SHOW ME THE BACK DOOR INSTEAD, BEFORE MY ARMS FALL OFF!

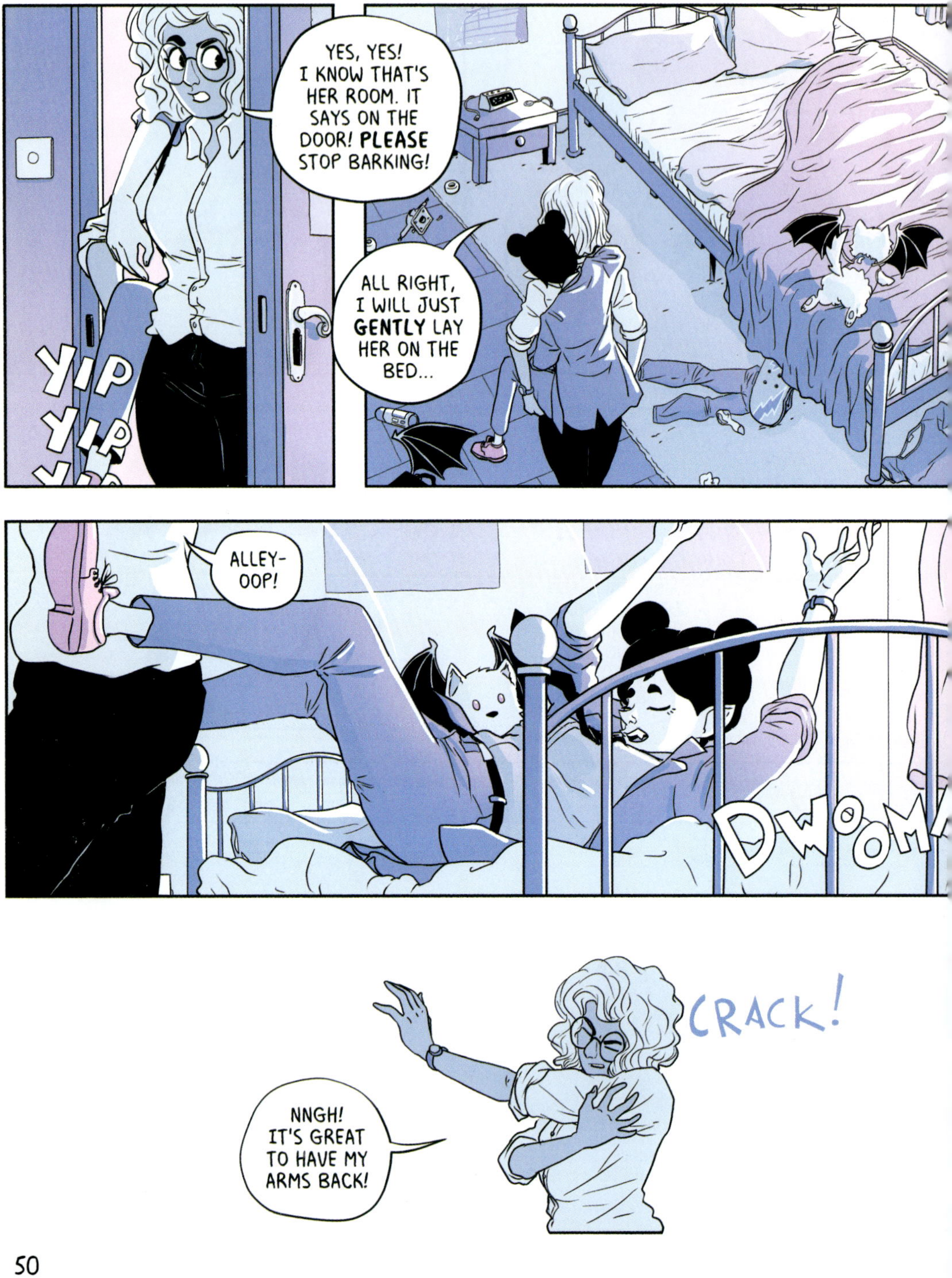

YES, YES! I KNOW THAT'S HER ROOM. IT SAYS ON THE DOOR! **PLEASE** STOP BARKING!

YIP

YIP

ALL RIGHT, I WILL JUST **GENTLY** LAY HER ON THE BED...

ZZZZ

THANKS FOR KIDNAPPING ME, VAMPIRE GIRL.

STOP FLIRTING WITZH MHR... ZZZ...

HEH!

SKRITCH SKRITCH

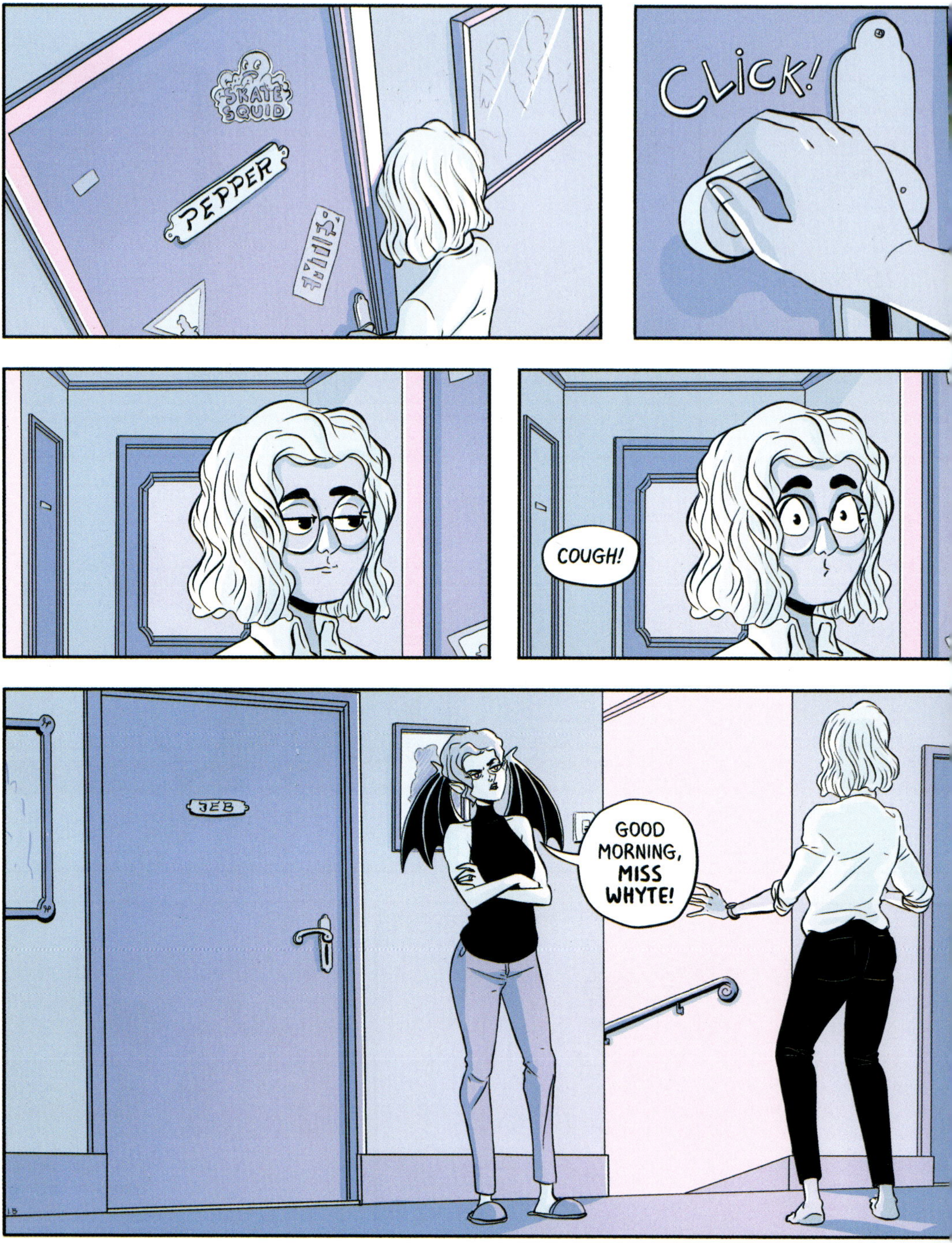

JEB

GOOD MORNING, MISS WHYTE!

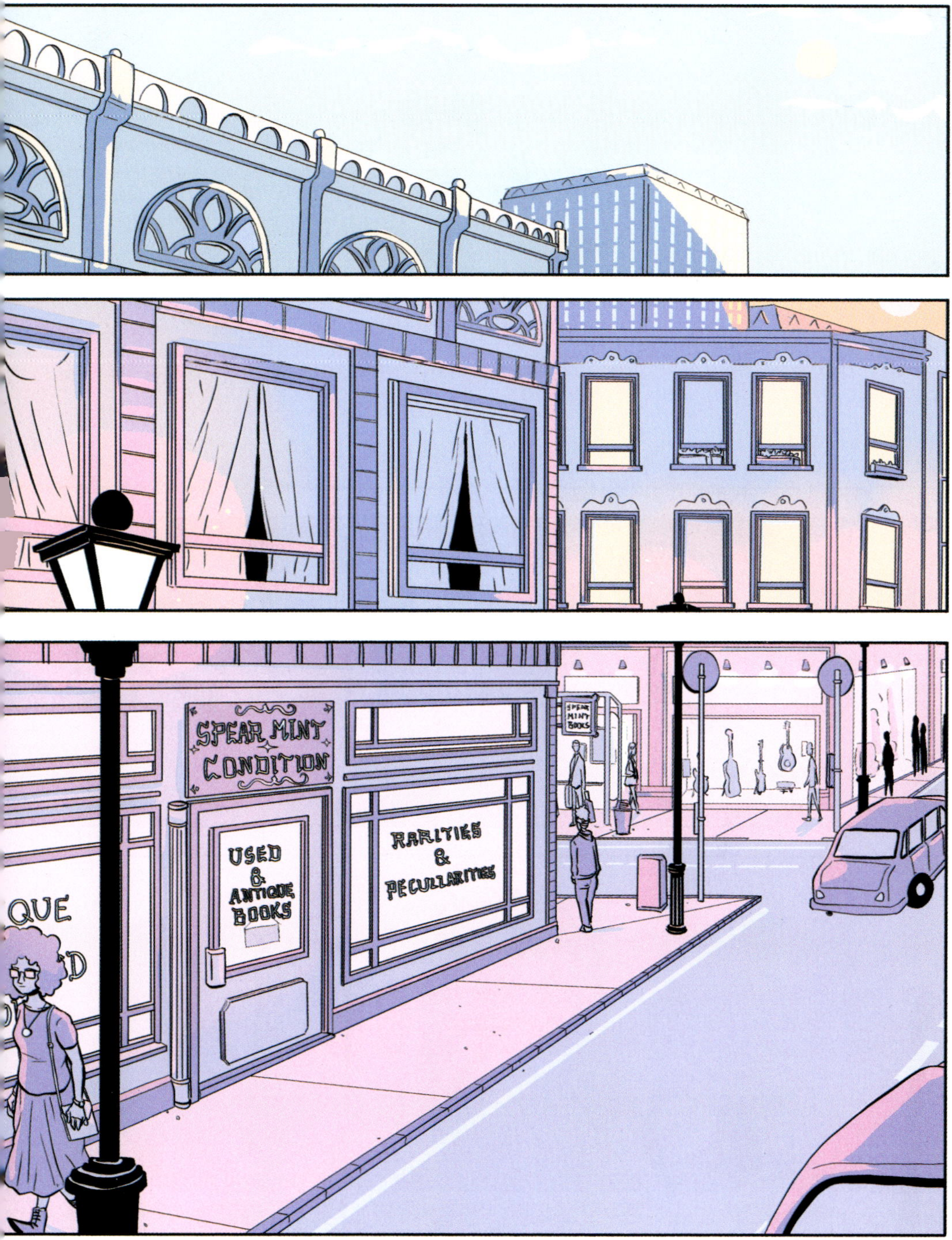

SPEAR MINT CONDITION
USED & ANTIQUE BOOKS
RARITIES & PECULIARITIES

ZZZ

B+
FOR VAMPIRES
EST 1986

B+
FOR VAMPIRES
EST 1986
B+
FOR VAMPIRES
EST 1986

SLAMM!
PFFFT
MOM! WHAT TIME IS IT? **NO!** WHAT **DAY** IS IT?

GOOD EVENENING TO YOU, AS WELL, PEPPER.

EVENING! OKAY! SAME DAY? HOW LONG HAVE I BEEN ASLEEP?
NO, **WAIT!** HOW DID I GET HOME?

SAME DAY, YES. YOU'VE BEEN OUT FOR ABOUT TWELVE HOURS, SO I ASSUME YOU HAVEN'T SLEPT FOR TWO OR THREE DAYS, AND SKIPPED ON THE B+ JUICE AS WELL.

NO, I MEAN **MAYBE,** BUT THAT'S BESIDE THE POINT! HOW DID I GET HOME?

BY THE LOOKS OF IT, YOUR FRIEND CARRIED YOU ACROSS TOWN TO MAKE SURE YOU WERE SAFE.
ANA? SHE DID?

WELL, THAT WAS BEFORE SHE REALIZED YOU COST HER HER JOB.
GULP!

WAIT!
DID YOU HAVE ANYTHING TO DO WITH IT?

NOW, WHY WOULD YOU THINK THAT?

BECAUSE IT WOULD BE **SO** TYPICALLY YOU!
PUNISHING ME WOULD BE EMBARRASSING IF ANYONE IN THE VAMPIRE COMMUNITY LEARNED ABOUT IT, BUT FLAUNTING YOUR INFLUENCE TO GET SOME POOR MORTAL FIRED IS A POWER MOVE BY YOUR STANDARDS.
YOU SEEM TO THINK VERY LITTLE OF ME, PEPPER.
MISS WHYTE GOT FIRED BY HER BOSS, WHO WAS ALREADY PRETTY PISSED AT HER FOR SOME REASON.

AND YOUR LITTLE ESCAPE STUNT, INCLUDING A **VERY** CONCUSSED PARTY GUEST, DID **PLENTY** TO EMBARRASS ME ALREADY.

BUT... WAIT! HOW DO YOU KNOW SHE CARRIED ME HOME?
AND HER SURNAME! DID YOU MEET HER?
DID YOU DO SOMETHING TO HER?

YES, PEPPER. I DID AND I DID.

CLACK!

I'VE HIRED HER.
OH! HEY, PEPPER!

SPEAR MINT CONDITION
USED & ANTIQUE BOOKS
RARITIES & PECULIARITIES
WHAT?

IS... SOMETHING WRONG?
N... NO?

OF COURSE NOT!
AS I EXPLAINED TO MISS WHYTE BEFORE, I FELT BAD THAT MY DAUGHTER'S ACTIONS CAUSED HER TO LOSE HER JOB, SO I DECIDED TO OFFER HER A PART-TIME SALES ASSISTANT POSITION IN THE SHOP. WHICH SHE ACCEPTED.
AND **VERY MUCH** APPRECIATED!

THAT... **IS** INDEED VERY NICE OF YOU, MOM.

AND ALSO A BIT SUSPICIOUS.

YOU HAVE SOME ULTERIOR MOTIVES, I BET!

INDEED, MY EVIL PLAN IS TO HIRE AN ASSISTANT WHO **ACTUALLY** WANTS TO WORK HERE, **UNLIKE** MY OWN DAUGHTER, SO I CAN HAVE SOME FREE TIME AND ALSO FOCUS ON OUR ONLINE SALES.

THAT'S THE FIRST TIME I'VE HEARD OF THIS. SINCE WHEN DO YOU KNOW ANYTHING ABOUT THE INTERNET?

I KNOW **PLENTY,** THANK YOU VERY MUCH!

ERR...

TO TRAIN MISS WHYTE.

WHAT?

I THINK THAT'S THE **LEAST** YOU CAN DO AFTER ALL THE TROUBLE YOU CAUSED. NOT TO MENTION SLEEPING THROUGH A WHOLE DAY WHILE I CLEANED UP YOUR MESS!

SLAMM!
UMM... PEPPER? IS THERE A PROBLEM?
SHE IS PLANNING SOMETHING.

I DUNNO. SHE WAS PRETTY NICE WHEN SHE CAUGHT ME **LITERALLY** SNEAKING OUT OF YOUR ROOM IN THE MORNING.
YIKES!
THAT WAS MY FIRST THOUGHT AS WELL. BUT THEN WE HAD A NICE CHAT, AND SHE SAID SHE JUST WISHES YOU DIDN'T MAKE A BIG FUSS AT THE PARTY, BUT SHE IS ALWAYS IN FAVOR OF YOU HAVING NEW FRIENDS.

OF COURSE SHE IS! SHE IS ALWAYS LOOKING FOR NEW PEOPLE SHE CAN HOOK ME UP WITH!
WELL, EVEN IF THAT WAS HER SECRET PLAN, I STILL NEEDED A NEW JOB, AND I COULD IMAGINE A WORSE WORK ENVIRONMENT THAN A BOOKSHOP WHERE THE OWNER WANTS ME TO BE PART OF HER FAMILY.

SIGH...
I... I KNOW, SORRY. YOU ARE RIGHT! THIS WAS VERY NICE OF HER, AND YOU DESERVE A NICE, CHILL JOB.
I SHOULD ACTUALLY GET TO IT AND TRAIN YOU UP.
OH, THAT? DON'T BOTHER. I'VE ALREADY FIGURED MOST OF IT OUT. I'VE WORKED IN RETAIL AND A LIBRARY BEFORE.

WHISTLE
WELL... MY JOB IS DONE HERE THEN, I GUESS?
ACTUALLY... I MIGHT NEED YOU FOR A...
THING.

A THING?

NOTHING DODGY. IT'S JUST A BIT... EMBARRASSING.

OH?

OKAY, SO...AFTER I TALKED TO YOUR MOM, BUT BEFORE I CAME BACK HERE FOR MY FIRST SHIFT, I HAD A CLASS.

I WAS DEAD TIRED AND COULDN'T FOCUS, SO I STARTED DOODLING.

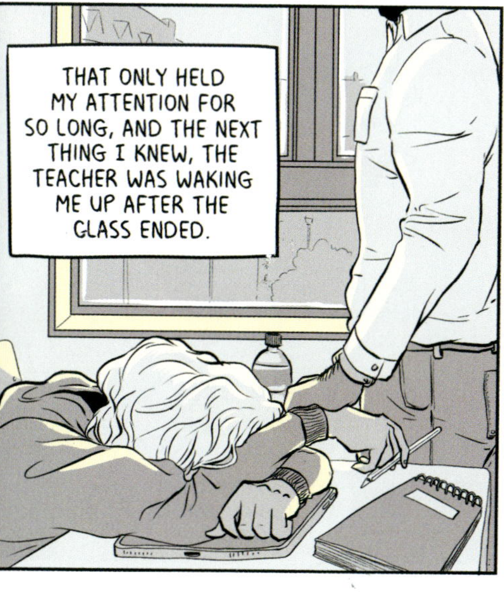
THAT ONLY HELD MY ATTENTION FOR SO LONG, AND THE NEXT THING I KNEW, THE TEACHER WAS WAKING ME UP AFTER THE CLASS ENDED.

WHEN I LIFTED MY HEAD UP FROM MY TABLET, HE NOTICED THE DRAWINGS AND ASKED ME ABOUT THEM.

IT WAS DRAWINGS OF VAMPIRES. AND A **SKATEBOARDING** ONE SPECIFICALLY.

YOU WERE RIGHT. IT **IS** EMBARRASSING, HE-HEHH!

WELL, HE DIDN'T THINK SO.

ACTUALLY, HE WAS VERY INTERESTED IN THE CONCEPT. THE CONTRAST AND SYNERGY BETWEEN A CREATURE OF THE NIGHT AND A STREET SPORT.
NEVER THOUGHT MY EXISTENCE WOULD BE SO NUANCED.

I **KNEW** THERE WAS SOMETHING EXTRA TO YOU. I JUST COULDN'T PUT MY FINGER ON WHAT, UNTIL HE SAID I SHOULD BASE THIS YEAR'S PROJECT ON **YOU**!
OH WOW. THESE ARE GREAT, BUT... I DON'T WEAR MY BAT-PACK WHILE I SKATE
MAYBE YOU **SHOULD**! IT WOULD LOOK **SO COOL**!

SURE, SURE, BUT MORE IMPORTANTLY...
DOES THIS MEAN YOU WANT ME TO MODEL FOR YOU?

KINDA? I WANT TO JUST DRA--

YOU WANT TO...

HUPP!

DRAW ME LIKE ONE OF YOUR FRENCH GIRLS?

HAHA! YOU SHOULD SEE YOUR FACE!

DING DEENG
YOU DON'T GET IT. THAT SCENE WAS--

HEY, IT'S ME. I GOT THE MES--

YOU KNOW WHAT? NONE OF MY BUSINESS! WELCOME TO THE TEAM, ANA!

IF ANYONE NEEDS ME, WHICH IS **NO ONE,** I KNOW, I KNOW, I WILL BE IN MY ROOM.

?

OH! **INTERESTING!** YOU ARE AN ARTIST! CAN I SEE?
UM... YEAH? SURE.

WELL, THAT'S HIM GONE TO SPIN A JUICY TALE ABOUT US TO MOM.

YEAH, I WAS THINKING MAYBE WE SHOULD BE DOING ACTUAL SKATEBOARD STUDIES FROM NOW ON? AND DO THEM...**NOT** IN THE SHOP?

RARITIES & PECURITIES

GOOD IDEA.

DWOOMM!

NICE!
THANKS!

SKWWSHH

HECK YEAH, GREG!
WOO!
YEE!
BAKK! BAKK!
THAKK!

WHAT HAPPENED?
GREG LANDED A **BACKSIDE LIPSLIDE!**

WHICH ONE IS THAT AGAIN?
THAT'S WHEN THE RAIL IS BEHIND YOU AND YOU DO A SLIDE WITH THE MIDDLE OF THE BOARD, BUT YOU SAID IT LOOKS BACKWARD AND COUNTER-INTUITIVE.

ISN'T THAT THE SAME THIN YOU DID JUST A FEW MINUTES AGO? WHY DID NO ONE CLAP FOR YOU THEN?

WELL...
WELL, **WHAT,** STEVE?

YOU, KNOW... THE **VAMPIRE** THING?
NO, PLEASE, STEVE, EXPLAIN IT WITH YOUR OWN WORDS. I HAVEN'T HEARD THIS NONSENSE IN A WHILE.

I THINK I'VE OPENED A CAN OF WORMS THAT I DIDN'T MEAN TO.
IT'S NOT NONSENSE, JUST **FACTS!** YOU ARE A VAMPIRE, SO YOU HAVE AN UNFAIR ADVANTAGE.
WHEN YOU DO A COOL TRICK, IT'S JUST NOT THAT SPECIAL, 'CAUSE YOU AR LIKE...**EXTRA** FIT.

WAIT, I THOUGHT YOU ARE NOT **THAT** IT UNTIL YOUR RNING. AND ISN'T KATEBOARDING BOUT TECHNICAL KILLS ANYWAY?
THAT'S WHAT I KEEP SAYING!

THEN WHY ARE YOU SO MUCH BETTER THAN ALL THE REST OF THE SKATERS HERE?

I DON'T NOW, MAN, **AYBE** I'M UST THAT OOD? HAVE OU EVER THOUGHT OF THAT?
MAYBE IF YOU PUT IN SOME EFFORT YOU COULD LAND A FLIP EVERY ONCE IN A WHILE AS WELL!
OKAY, THEN WHY DON'T YOU COMPETE?

'CAUSE THEY CLASSED MY **B+ JUICE** AS DOPING, EVEN THOUGH I LITERALLY HAVE TO DRINK IT SO I WON'T FALL ASLEEP DURING THE DAY!
I'M NOT EVEN **FULLY** A VAMPIRE YET!
I MEAN... YOU GOT THE FANGS AND THE EARS...

THUD!
STEVE, YOU MAKE US SOUND LIKE JERKS IN FRONT OF PEPPER'S **GIRLFRIEND!**
IT'S NOT LIKE WE DON'T LIKE HER!
UMM, SOPHIE, NO, WE DON--

OH, I'M, HAHA...WE **AREN'T** DATING! WE ARE JUST COWORKERS.

OH, SORRY, JUST 'CAUSE YOU WERE ONLY FILMING HER, SO WE THOUGHT...
IT'S 'CAUSE I'M DOING A PROJECT ON HER FOR MY COLLEGE COURSE.

A WHOLE PROJECT? ON **PEPPER?**

NO... WELL, YEAH... WELL, I DON'T KNOW.
IT'S AN ART PROJECT. I STUDY ILLUSTRATION, AND MY TEACHER SAW MY SKETCHES OF PEPPER SKATEBOARDING, AND WE AGREED THAT A VAMPIRE SKATEBOARDER HAS SOME POTENTIAL.
WEIRD, 'CAUSE AS STEVE JUST SAID, PEOPLE USUALLY DON'T FIND VAMPIRE SKATEBOARDERS THAT INTERESTING.

MAYBE NOT FROM A SPORTS PERSPECTIVE. BUT I'M APPROACHING IT FROM A VISUAL ANGLE.
PEOPLE TEND TO ASSOCIATE VAMPIRES WITH GOTHIC-INSPIRED HORROR...
WHILE SKATEBOARDING IS MORE OF AN URBAN SPORT, DEVELOPED FAIRLY RECENTLY WITH ROOTS IN HIP-HOP AND ROCK.
I THINK IT CREATES AN INTERESTING JUXTAPOSITION THAT IS STILL A COHERENT IMAGE.
I CAN'T QUITE PUT MY FINGER ON **WHY** YET, BUT I FIND IT COMPELLING.
HUH...
HUH, INDEED! ARTISTS ALWAYS BAFFLED ME, BUT I HAVE TO ADMIT, YOU HAVE A POINT. I ALWAYS LIKED THE LOOK OF THOSE **BAT WINGS.**
DO YOU LIKE THEM ENOUGH TO WEAR THEM YOURSELF?

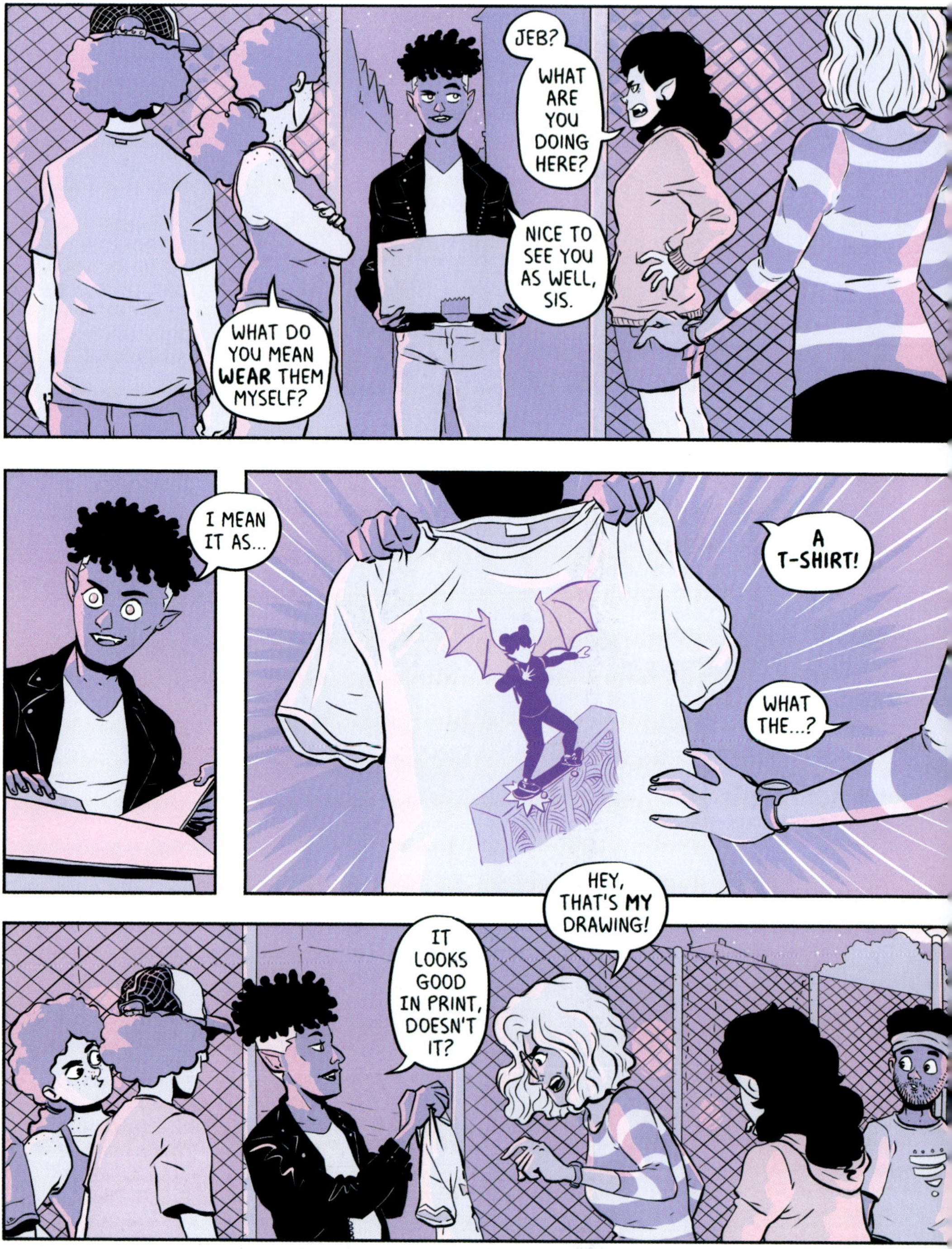

JEB?
WHAT ARE YOU DOING HERE?
NICE TO SEE YOU AS WELL, SIS.
WHAT DO YOU MEAN **WEAR** THEM MYSELF?

I MEAN IT AS...
A T-SHIRT!
WHAT THE...?

IT LOOKS GOOD IN PRINT, DOESN'T IT?
HEY, THAT'S **MY** DRAWING!

YOU DESIGNED THIS, ANA? IT LOOKS **SICK!**
AND IT'S **FREE!**
I'LL TAKE ONE IF IT'S FREE!
ME TOO!
I GOT SOME HATS AS WELL!
HEY, I DIDN'T AGREE TO **ANY** OF THIS!
DID YOU LITERALLY **STEAL** MY ART AND MAKE IT INTO **MERCH?**
ALSO, ISN'T THIS, LIKE... LIKE, IDENTITY THEFT OR SOMETHING?
OKAY, OKAY! LET ME EXPLAIN BEFORE YOU BITE MY HEAD OFF, PLEASE!
THIS IS A GOOD THING. JUST HEAR ME OUT, OKAY?

YES, I DID SORTA KINDA TAKE YOUR ART WITHOUT YOUR PERMISSION WHEN I SAID I WOULD SHOW IT TO MOM. AND I DID PUT IT ON SHIRTS AND HATS. BUT I DID IT TO PROVE A POINT!
AND IT'S THE EXACT SAME POINT YOU WERE JUST MAKING!
GREAT MINDS THINK ALIKE!

I'M DOING A COLLEGE PROJECT, AND YOU ARE STEALING IT TO PUT IT ON MERCH.
HOW IS THAT EXACTLY "THINKING ALIKE"?
BECAUSE WE BOTH SAW THE POTENTIAL IN THIS VISUAL HERE! THE SAME THING YOU JUST EXPLAINED A MINUTE AGO!
THE WEIRDLY COMPELLING CONTRAST BETWEEN THE SPORT AND THE AESTHETIC!

EXCEPT YOU TURNED IT INTO ART! AND I...
WILL TURN IT INTO MONEY!
I KNEW IT! HERE COMES THE GRIFT AGAIN!
MONEY? YOU MEAN YOU WANT TO SELL THESE?

NO, THESE ARE JUST THE TEST SAMPLES. THAT'S WHY I'M GIVING THEM AWAY FOR FREE!
AND DON'T CALL IT A **GRIFT**, PEPPER! THIS IS A **BUSINESS** INVESTMENT!

IF **YOU** ARE DOING IT, IT'S A GRIFT.

AND THIS ATTITUDE IS THE **EXACT** REASON WHY **I** ALWAYS HAVE MONEY, AND **YOU** HAVE TO WORK IN THE SHOP WITHOUT ANY FUTURE PLANS, JUST SO YOU CAN AFFORD NEW SKATE GEAR.
OH, SORRY, MISTER RICH BUSINESSMAN, WHO LIVES IN THE ROOM OPPOSITE FROM MINE IN HIS MOMMA'S HOUSE!

YEAH? WELL...

YOU KNOW WHAT? NO!
I WILL PROVE TO YOU THAT I'M SERIOUS, AND WILL **NOT** ENGAGE IN A CHILDISH SPITTING CONTEST.

HOW MUCH MONEY ARE WE TALKING ABOUT?
WHAT?

PEPPER, I'M AN ARTIST. I'M **ALWAYS** BROKE, AND I WANT TO BE PAID FOR MY WORK.

YES! THAT'S THE RIGHT ATTITUDE!
AND I PROMISE YOU **COMPLETE** TRANSPARENCY FROM NOW ON!
JUST TELL US YOUR PLAN, JEB.

IT'S SIMPLE! WE CREATE A **SKATEBOARD BRAND** BASED ON YOUR IDEA OF MIXING VAMPIRES AND SPORTS!
IT'S A NOVEL IDEA, ALL THREE OF US HAVE SOMETHING TO CONTRIBUTE, AND, AS YOU CAN SEE, THE KIDS WERE **ALL OVER IT** ALREADY!
OF COURSE THEY WERE! YOU JUST GAVE THEM SOME FREE SHIRTS AND HATS!

BUT THEY LIKED THE DESIGNS! THEY DON'T SEE PEPPER ON THEM. THEY SEE THE WINGS AND THE COOL ART. THE FACT THAT IT WAS FREE IS JUST A BONUS.
AND ONLY THE FIRST TASTE IS FREE!
HMM...

OH, COME ON! AND WHY DOES IT HAVE TO BE THE **DARN WINGS?**
IT'S ALREADY HARD TO BE TAKEN SERIOUSLY AS A SKATEBOARDER **WITHOUT** CALLING ATTENTION TO THE WINGS!

IT'S ONLY THE **ONE** IMAGE, PEPPER. WE CAN COME UP WITH A BUNCH OF OTHER COOL DESIGNS.

AND THINK OF ALL THE SKATEBOARDING GEAR YOU CAN BUY YOURSELF **WITHOUT** HAVING TO PUT IN EXTRA HOURS IN THE SHOP, HELPING MOM.

SIGH!

OKAY, WHAT'S YOUR PLAN?
AND WHAT'S OUR CUT?

YESSS! I **KNEW** THIS WAS A GOOD IDEA!

NOW WE JUST NEED TO COME UP WITH A BRAND NAME AND SOME DESIGNS TO START OUT WITH.

I ALREADY HAVE A FEW IDEAS AND THEY'RE ALL CERTIFIED BANGERS!

SHOULDN'T TAKE LONGER THAN A FEW HOURS OF BRAINSTORMING, AND WE WILL BE **READY TO ROLL!**

2 WEEKS LATER.

I **MIGHT** HAVE UNDERESTIMATED THE COMPLEXITY OF THIS TASK.
bite
skate with a bloodlust!
WELL, YEAH, IT TOOK US **SOME** EFFORT, BUT THIS IS IT, RIGHT?
YES! PLEASE!
Z Z Z

THEN, I WOULD LIKE TO ANNOUNCE...
THAT OUR BRAND IS OFFICIALLY NOW CALLED...
bite
skate with a bloodlust!
BITE!
TAGLINE: "SKATE WITH A BLOODLUST!"
I STILL THINK WE SHOULD LEAVE THE TAGLINE OUT. IT'S JUST PANDERING TO A HARMFUL STEREOTYPE.
YEAH, BUT IT'S ABOUT SKATEBOARDING, NOT MURDERING PEOPLE. YOU **HAVE TO** PANDER TO YOUR AUDIENCE A BIT.
MOST OF OUR CUSTOMERS WILL BE EDGY TEENS, AND THEY EAT THIS TYPE OF STUFF UP!
bite
skate with a bloodlust!
ALSO, WE WILL AVOID DEPICTING **ACTUAL** BLOOD, AND FOCUS MORE ON THE WINGS AND THE FANGS. AT LEAST UNTIL WE ESTABLISH OURSELVES A BIT ON THE MARKET.

YEAH, THAT'S THE OTHER THING! I THOUGHT WE WERE GOING TO COOL DOWN WITH ALL THE **BAT WING** STUFF!
I REMEMBER **SPECIFICALLY** REQUESTING IT!
BECAUSE YOU LACK VISION.
YOU ARE GOING TO BE AN AMBASSADOR FOR ALL VAMPIRES, WHO ARE OVERLOOKED BY HUMANS!

AND IT'S NOT REALLY ABOUT THE WINGS! ALL THREE OF THE STARTING DESIGNS ARE BASED ON TRICKS!
THE SLIDE!
GRAVE GRIND
FIRST THING I SPOT ON THIS ARE THE WINGS!

THE FLIP!
COFFIN FLIP
THE WINGS ARE EVEN BIGGER THIS TIME!

AND THE BIG JUMP!
THIS ONE JUST LOOKS LIKE I'M STRAIGHT-UP FLYING!
AND IT'S CALLED AN **OLLIE!**

I KNOW YOU JANT TO BE SEEN A SKATEBOARDER, JT GOOD SKATERS E TWELVE A DOZEN UT THERE. BUT A AMPIRE ONE WHO LSO HAS A UNIQUE APPEARANCE?
YOU HAVE THE ADVANTAGE OF HAVING A **VERY COOL** MARKETABLE FEATURE ON TOP OF BEING GOOD AT THE SPORT.
AGREED! CAN'T WAIT TO S--
AH, THERE'S EVERYONE!

WE HAVE **FIVE MINUTES** TILL OPENING, AND I STILL HAVE A HUGE STACK OF NEW BOOKS TO SHELVE...

WHAT'S GOING ON HERE?

OH, UMM.. THAT'S THE NEW BUSINESS PLAN I WAS TELLING YOU ABOUT THE OTHER DAY.

IT'S...
IT'S A SKATEBOARD BRAND?
IT IS!

AND WHO DESIGNED THESE?

THAT WAS ME.
OH, OF COURSE! I'VE SEEN YOUR SKETCHES BEFORE. I JUST DIDN'T REALIZE YOU ARE THIS GOOD!

HEHE, THANKS!

WOW! EVEN PEPPER IS INVOLVED? IS SHE THE COMPANY MASCOT?

COUGH COUGH
I'M NOT A MASCOT! I'M THE COMPANY'S FIRST PRO SKATER!

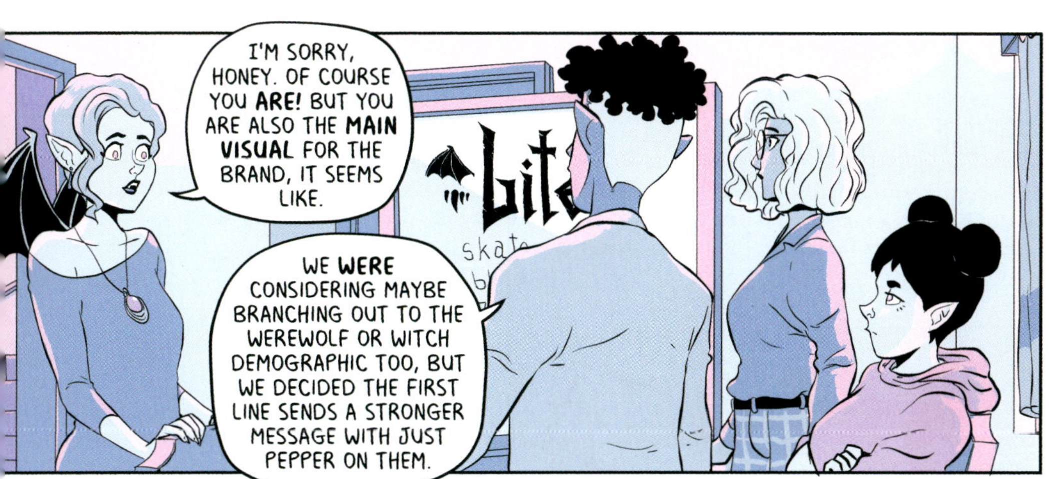
I'M SORRY, HONEY. OF COURSE YOU **ARE!** BUT YOU ARE ALSO THE **MAIN VISUAL** FOR THE BRAND, IT SEEMS LIKE.
WE **WERE** CONSIDERING MAYBE BRANCHING OUT TO THE WEREWOLF OR WITCH DEMOGRAPHIC TOO, BUT WE DECIDED THE FIRST LINE SENDS A STRONGER MESSAGE WITH JUST PEPPER ON THEM.

GOOD IDEA, BUT...HMM...
WHERE DO YOU GET THE MONEY FROM TO START PRODUCING YOUR FIRST LINE?

I WAS THINKING ABOUT SOME POTENTIAL INVESTORS.
WE WILL DO A SHOOT TOMORROW, AND THEN WE'RE GONNA SET UP A WEBSITE WITH MOCK-UP PRODUCTS, SO WE CAN START PITCHING OUR BRAND.

YOU SHOULD PITCH TO THE **HUMAN RELATIONS COUNCIL!**
THE WHO?
GRAVE

THEY ARE A GROUP OF VAMPIRES, MAINLY RICH BUSINESSPEOPLE, WHO WERE BORN VAMPIRES AND NEVER EXPERIENCED JUST BEING A HUMAN. SO THEY DEVELOPED A BIT OF AN OBSESSION WITH THEM.
AND THEY ARE ALWAYS LOOKING FOR OPPORTUNITIES TO FURTHER HUMAN-VAMPIRE RELATIONS.

AND YOU THINK THEY WOULD BE INTERESTED IN **US?**

OH YES! THE IMAGE OF A VAMPIRE IN THE CONTEXT OF A SPORT IT'S USUALLY NOT ASSOCIATED WITH?
IT SENDS A HOPEFUL MESSAGE TO YOUNG OR NEW VAMPIRES, THAT THEY CAN DO ANYTHING THEY WANT, EVEN IF THEY AREN'T HUMAN.
IT FEELS LIKE THIS IS A PROJECT **TAILOR-MADE** FOR THE COUNCIL. IT CAN HELP BOTH HUMANS AND VAMPIRES, **AND** MAKE QUITE A BIT OF MONEY AS WELL.

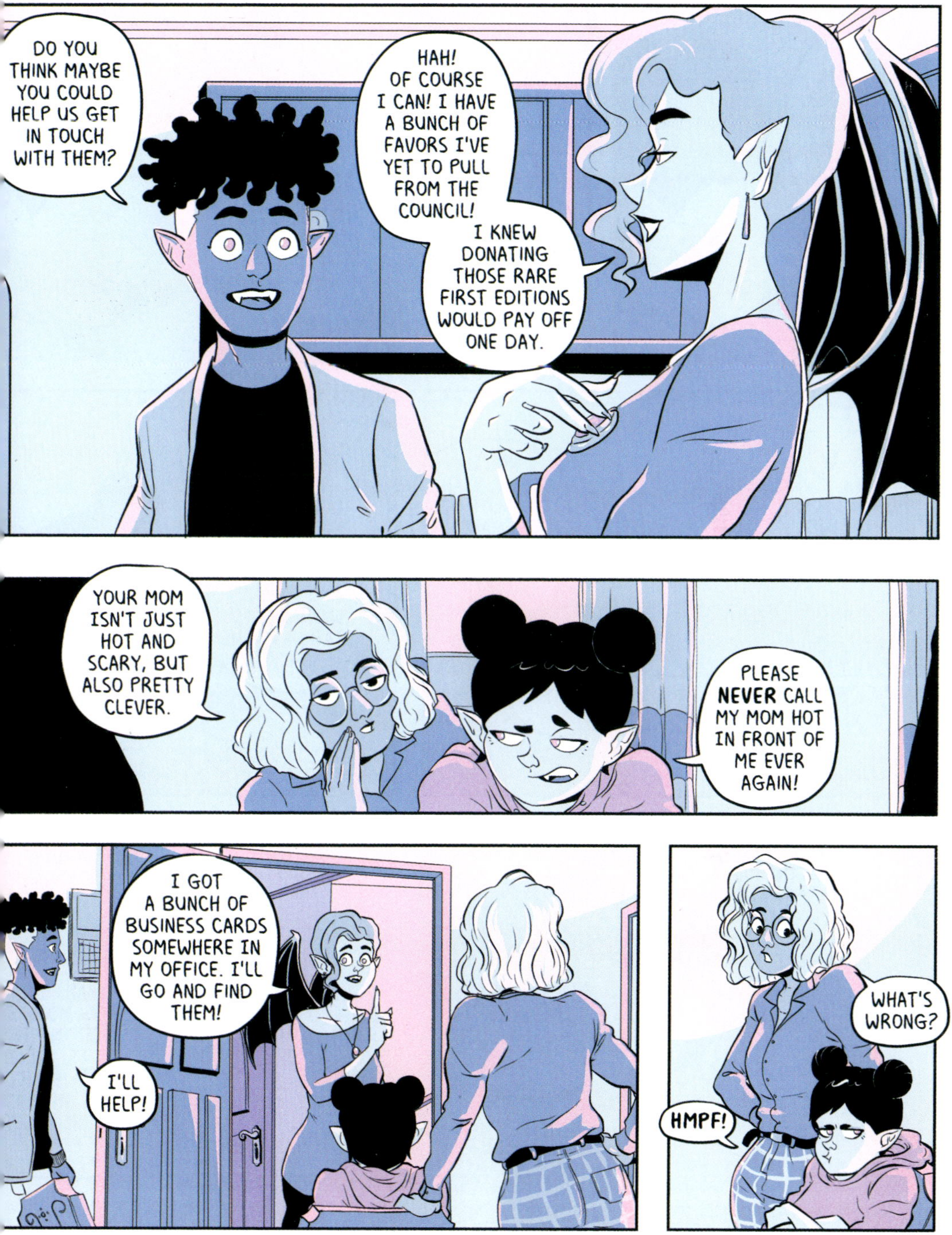

DO YOU THINK MAYBE YOU COULD HELP US GET IN TOUCH WITH THEM?
HAH! OF COURSE I CAN! I HAVE A BUNCH OF FAVORS I'VE YET TO PULL FROM THE COUNCIL!
I KNEW DONATING THOSE RARE FIRST EDITIONS WOULD PAY OFF ONE DAY.

FIRST WE TEAM UP WITH JEB, AND NOW MOM IS GETTING INVOLVED AS WELL.

AND?

I JUST... DON'T LIKE IT.

YOU DON'T LIKE YOUR FAMILY HELPING OUT?
NO...I... OKAY, YEAH, I REALIZE HOW THAT MAKES ME SOUND.

BUT I DON'T TRUST JEB. HE IS TOO MUCH OF AN OPPORTUNIST, AND I DON'T WANT HIM TO STAB US IN THE BACK.

bloodlust
WE DID THE PAPERWORK FOR THE COMPANY TOGETHER, PEPPER. AND WE MADE SURE THAT **CAN'T** HAPPEN.
YEAH, BUT NOW MOM IS GETTING IN ON IT, AND I ALWAYS FEEL LIKE SHE HAS A SCHEME SET UP FOR ME.

PEPPER, YOUR MOM IS JUST HAPPY FOR YOU AND TRYING TO HELP.
THAT'S WHAT MOMS ARE SUPPOSED TO DO.

NOT THAT I KNOW IT FROM EXPERIENCE, SO I MIGHT BE WRONG.

ANA... I...

IT'S OKAY. LET'S GO AND OPEN THE SHOP. THEN WE CAN PLAN OUT THE PHOTO SHOOT. ALL RIGHT?

ALL RIGHT...

NEXT DAY.

SIGH...

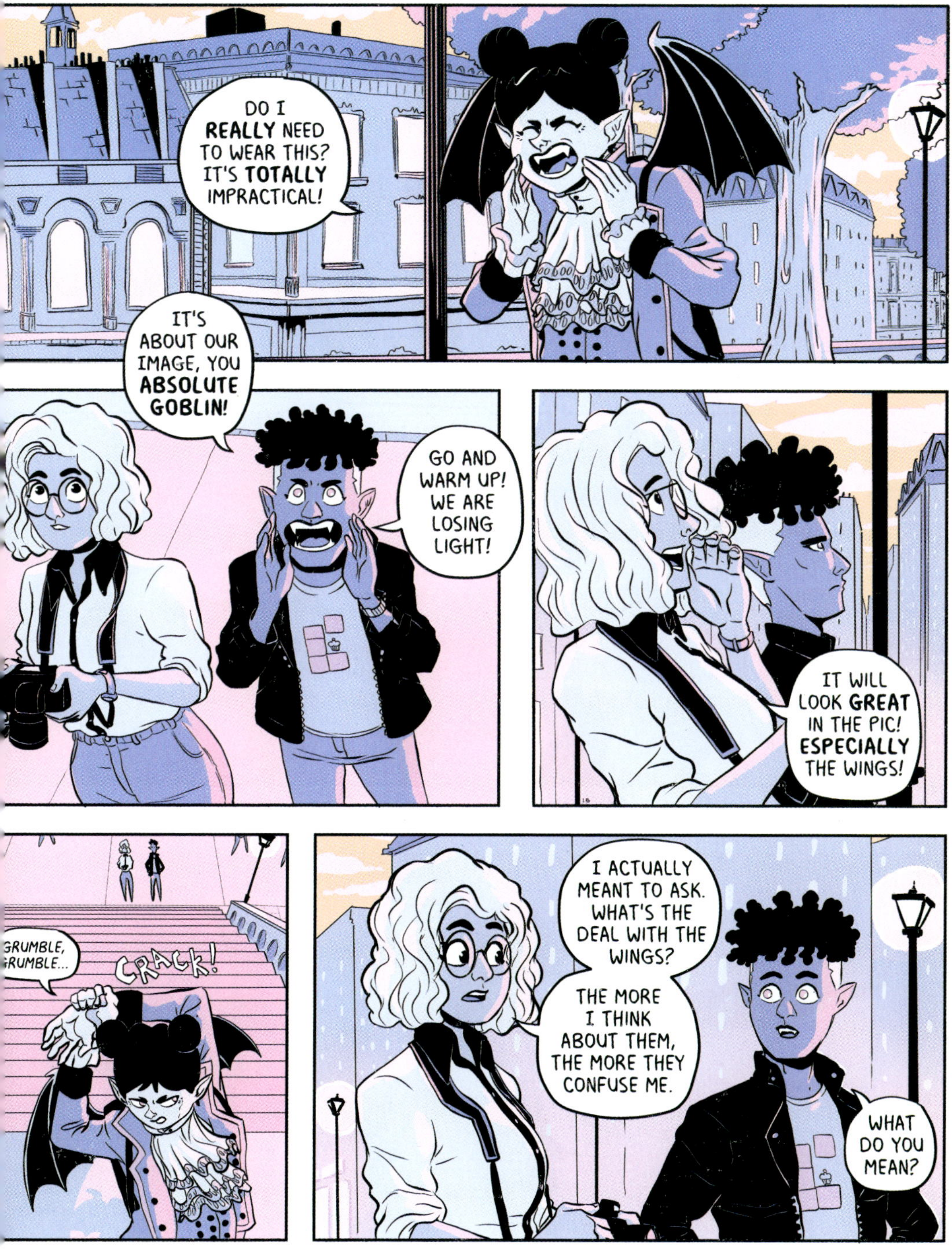

DO I **REALLY** NEED TO WEAR THIS? IT'S **TOTALLY** IMPRACTICAL!

IT'S ABOUT OUR IMAGE, YOU **ABSOLUTE GOBLIN!**

GO AND WARM UP! WE ARE LOSING LIGHT!

IT WILL LOOK **GREAT** IN THE PIC! **ESPECIALLY** THE WINGS!

SHE HAD A LOT OF OBJECTIONS INCLUDING THEM IN THE DESIGNS, AND WEARING THEM TODAY.
BUT SHE DOES WEAR THE BACKPACK BASICALLY EVERYWHERE. SO SHE CLEARLY DOESN'T HATE IT **THAT MUCH.**
ALSO, COULD SHE NOT JUST GROW WINGS LIKE YOUR MOM?

I DON'T REALLY KNOW WHAT EXACTLY IS GOING ON IN HER HEAD.
BUT I THINK SHE ACTUALLY ALWAYS WANTED TO HAVE THE WINGS.

I CAN CLEARLY REMEMBER HER BRINGING IT UP ALL THE TIME WHEN WE WERE LITTLE.
MOM! MOM!

WHAT, DARLING?
I WANT WINGS LIKE YOURS, MOM! SO I CAN FLY WITH THE BATS!

YOU WILL BE ABLE TO GROW THEM OUT AFTER YOUR TURNING.
BUT WHEN IS THE TURNIN' GOING TO HAPPEN?
MAYBE ANOTHER TEN YEARS? WHEN YOU ARE FULLY GROWN AND READY TO HAVE A BRIDE.

TEN YEARS? BOO! THAT'S, LIKE...**FOREVER!**
I WANT THE WINGS **NOW!**

SIGH...

SHOULD'VE SEEN PEPPER'S FACE WHEN SHE GOT THE **BAT-PACK** FOR HER TENTH BIRTHDAY. MOM SPENT A FORTUNE ON GETTING IT CUSTOM-MADE BY A WITCH.
BUT I GUESS THE WINGS STUCK AS A CHILDHOOD MEMENTO.
HER RESENTING THE TURNING STARTED AROUND THE TIME SHE GOT SERIOUS ABOUT SKATEBOARDING.
WHO WOULD'VE THOUGHT SHE WAS A MOMMA'S GIRL.

YEAH, WELL... PEPPER ALWAYS SAYS I'M MOM'S FAVORITE, BUT LOOK WHO GOT THE **CUSTOM MAGIC BACKPACK** FOR HER TENTH BIRTHDAY.

SO WHAT DID **YOU** GET FOR YOUR TENTH BIRTHDAY?

HEHH...

MY ADOPTION PAPERS.

HEY!

ARE WE DOING THIS OR **WHAT?**

YEAH, WE ARE READY. YOU CAN DO IT WHENEVER!

Slurp!

Exhale...
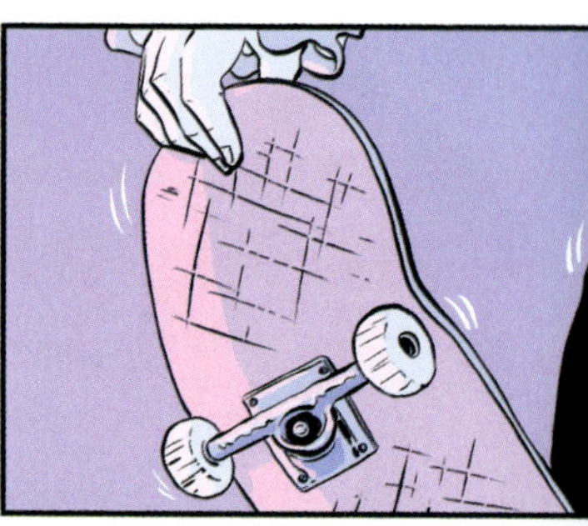

PAKK!
CLICK
CLICK
CLICK
CLICK
FWOOM!

THADD!
CLICK
CLICK
CLICK

SKRREE

NICE!

THAT LOOKED **GREAT**, PEPPER!

THANKS, I...

ALL RIGHT, LET'S GO, OR WE'LL BE LATE.

MOM! THAT WAS **AWESOME!**
I WANT WINGS TOO!
OH BOY!

ALL GOOD?
YEAH, LET'S GO BACK TO YOURS SO I CAN EDIT THESE AND PUT THE WEBPAGE TOGETHER.

PEPPER, YOU COMING?

SORRY, I ZONED OUT!

CROSS COUNTRY MAP TO THE UNIVERSE
D.A.
THE SMELL OF MAGIC
THE LIGHT QUITE IMPRESSIVE
HORRIBLE SQUADRON
AWKWARD BROTHERS
BOBY HICK
A WIZARD OF WATERSTONE
U.K. PENGUIN
GROWE'S ROLLING MANOR
GROWE'S ROLLING MANOR

HAVE A NICE DAY!
YOU TOO, THANKS!
HMM HMMM HM...

AND **NOTHING** TO DO WITH THE ADMIRING LOOKS OF A SMALL CHILD AFTER YOU'R BIG TRICK YESTERDAY?

PLEASE, YOU CAN WOW A SIX-YEAR-OLD WITH ANYTHING.

CLICK

ALL RIGHT, I WILL CALL YOU NEXT TIME I GET A SIDE GIG AS A BABY-SITTER, 'CAUSE I CANNOT COPE WITH THOSE LITTLE MONSTERS.

WELL, JUST ORDER THE SAME SUIT AGAIN, THEN!

YES, I MEANT TO DO THAT, BUT THEY ARE SOLD OUT IN YOUR SIZE, SO NOW WE NEED TO BUY A NEW ONE, TEE-HEE!

UUUGH! FINE!

SPEAR MINT CONDITION
RARITIES & PECULIARITIES
ANTIQUE & SECOND

DING DEENG

HI THERE! CAN I HELP WITH ANYTHING?

HEY, YEAH. MY NAME IS TED BROWN. I'M FROM THE **HUMAN RELATIONS COUNCIL.**
I'M LOOKING FOR A MISS ANA WHYTE.

OH, THAT'S ME! HI!

AH... **I SEE.**

YOU SOUND A BIT... DISAPPOINTED?
YOU HERE TO TALK ABOUT INVESTING IN **BITE**, RIGHT?
YES, FORGIVE ME. I JUST THOUGHT YOU WERE A...YOU KNOW...**A VAMPIRE.**
SINCE YOU WANTED TO DO BUSINESS WITH A **VAMPIRE COUNCIL.**

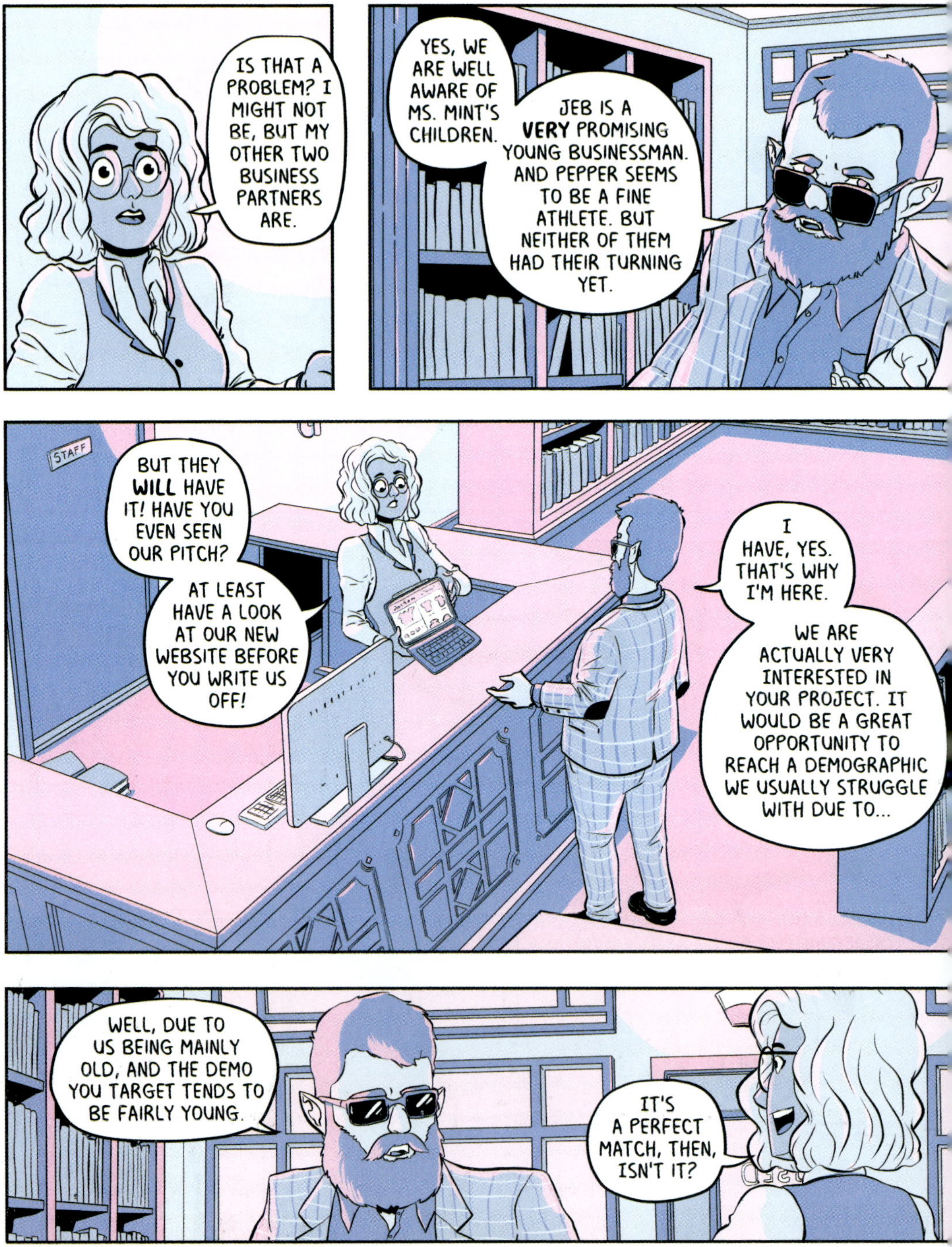

STAFF

BUT THEY **WILL** HAVE IT! HAVE YOU EVEN SEEN OUR PITCH?

AT LEAST HAVE A LOOK AT OUR NEW WEBSITE BEFORE YOU WRITE US OFF!

I HAVE, YES. THAT'S WHY I'M HERE.

WE ARE ACTUALLY VERY INTERESTED IN YOUR PROJECT. IT WOULD BE A GREAT OPPORTUNITY TO REACH A DEMOGRAPHIC WE USUALLY STRUGGLE WITH DUE TO...

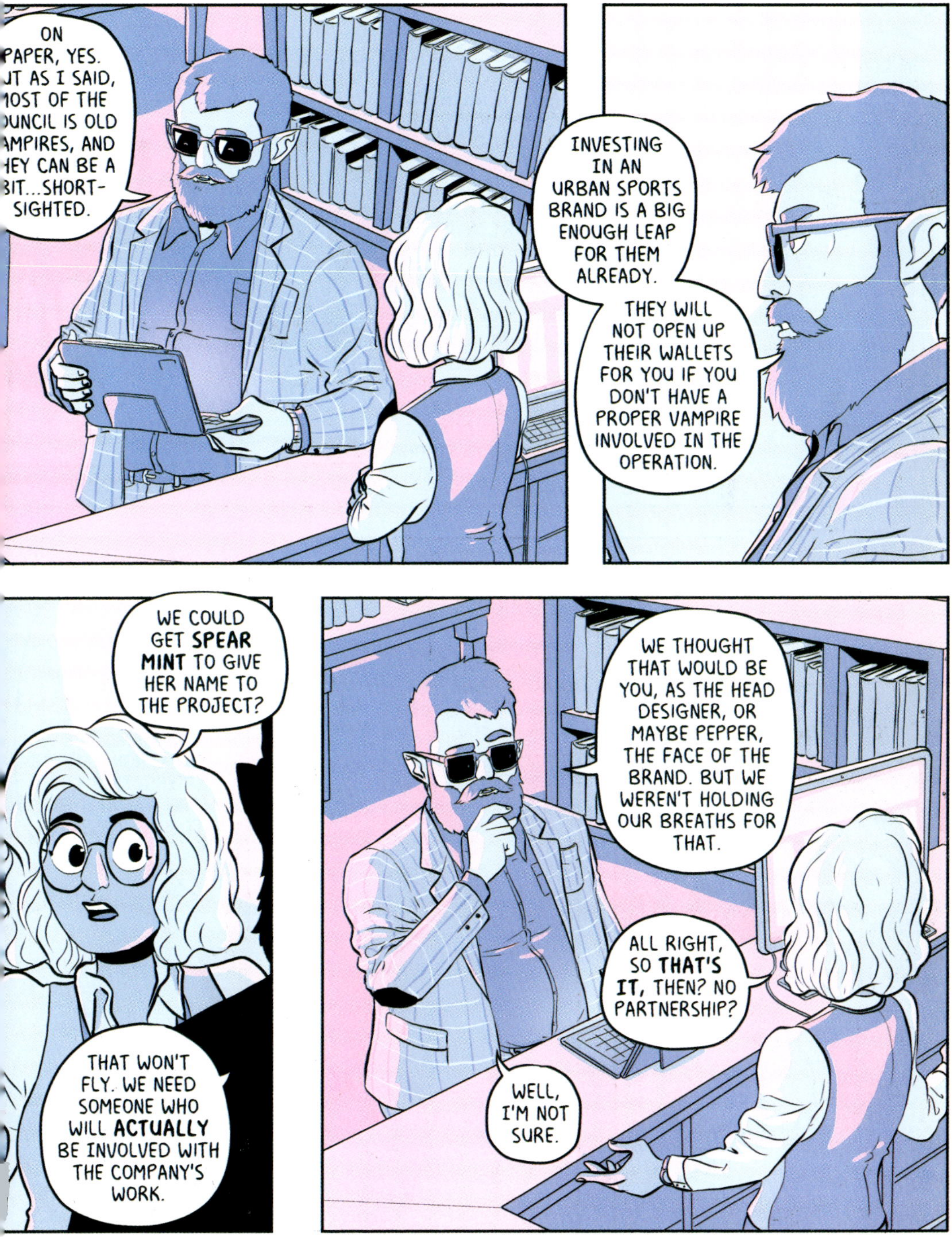

ON PAPER, YES. UT AS I SAID, OST OF THE UNCIL IS OLD AMPIRES, AND HEY CAN BE A IT...SHORT-SIGHTED.

INVESTING IN AN URBAN SPORTS BRAND IS A BIG ENOUGH LEAP FOR THEM ALREADY.

THEY WILL NOT OPEN UP THEIR WALLETS FOR YOU IF YOU DON'T HAVE A PROPER VAMPIRE INVOLVED IN THE OPERATION.

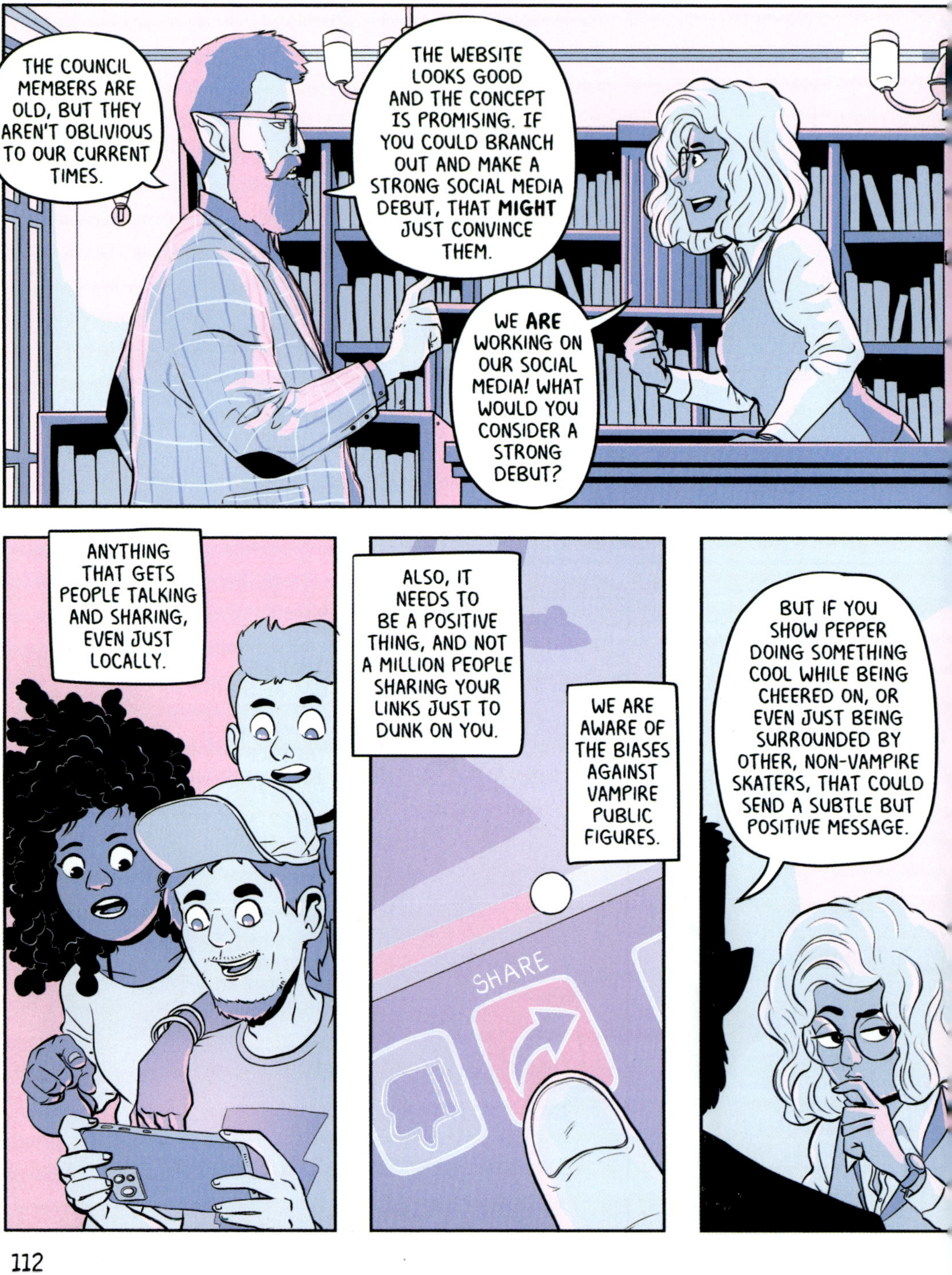

THE COUNCIL MEMBERS ARE OLD, BUT THEY AREN'T OBLIVIOUS TO OUR CURRENT TIMES.

THE WEBSITE LOOKS GOOD AND THE CONCEPT IS PROMISING. IF YOU COULD BRANCH OUT AND MAKE A STRONG SOCIAL MEDIA DEBUT, THAT **MIGHT** JUST CONVINCE THEM.

WE **ARE** WORKING ON OUR SOCIAL MEDIA! WHAT WOULD YOU CONSIDER A STRONG DEBUT?

SHE **DOES** HAVE HUMAN FRIENDS! THEY DO OVERLOOK HER EFFORTS, BUT THEY LIKE HER AS A PERSON.
GREAT! DO A VIDEO SHOOT WITH THEM. GET THEM TO WEAR YOUR MERCH, AND MAKE SURE AT LEAST ONE OF THEM CLAPS WHEN PEPPER DOES A COOL TRICK!
SPREAD THAT ONLINE, DO SOME FUNKY EDITS TO POPULAR SONGS, OR WHATEVER.
AND YOU THINK THAT'S GOING TO BE ENOUGH TO GET THE FUNDING FROM THE COUNCIL?
WELL, YOUR BEST BET WOULD BE MAKING THAT HAPPEN BY THE **GALA,** ALONG WITH AN ANNOUNCEMENT.
ABOUT WHAT?
WELL, THE GALA IS WHERE THE NEW **BRIDES** USUALLY GET ANNOUNCED AND GET THE BIGGEST ATTENTION.
I WILL LEAVE YOU TO FIGURE OUT THE REST. FOR LEGAL REASONS.

GOOD LUCK WITH THE PROMO!

SPEAR MINT CONDITION
ANTIQUE

CLICK
UGH! THAT WAS AN ABSOLUTE WASTE OF TIME AND MONEY.

IT'S THE **EXACT** SAME SUIT JUST A BIT OF A LIGHTER COLOR.
ANYWAY, BACK TO THE JOYS OF SHELVING BOOKS!

HMMM HM-HMM HMMM...

TAK
TAKKA
TAK

TAK
TAKKA
TAKTAK

OH, HEY! YOU TAKING A BREAK?

WE NEED TO TALK.

bite
bite

OKAY, EVERYONE! TRY TO SPREAD AROUND THE PARK A BIT! TWO OR THREE OF YOU AT THE SAME SPOT!
AND MAKE SURE **NOT** TO COVER UP OUR LOGO OR I'LL TAKE BACK THE FREE SHIRTS!
GRIND
ANA WILL GO AROUND IN A MINUTE AND SHOOT SOME B-ROLL FOOTAGE OF YOU GUYS, WHILE PEPPER GETS READY FOR THE **BIG JUMP**!
STRETCH
WISH YOU WOULD STOP CALLING IT THAT.

THE SOONER WE FINISH THIS, THE SOONER I WILL ORDER THE PIZZAS!

I APPRECIATE YOUR HELP, GUYS, EVEN IF IT'S FOR THE FREE FOOD

bite
DON'T SWEAT IT MAN. WE WERE ACTUALLY JUST TALKING ABOUT HOW IT'S PRETTY COOL TO HAVE A LOCAL BRAND. EVEN IF IT'S A FREAKY VAMPIRE ONE.
BUT YOU KNOW, IT'S **OUR** FREAKY VAMPIRE. JUST LIKE PEPPER.

OKAY, I THINK I JUST NEED A FEW MORE SHOTS OF YOU TWO, AND THEN WE CAN FINISH IT UP WITH PEPPER.

JUST A WORD, JEB.
DID YOU MENTION ANYTHING TO HER?

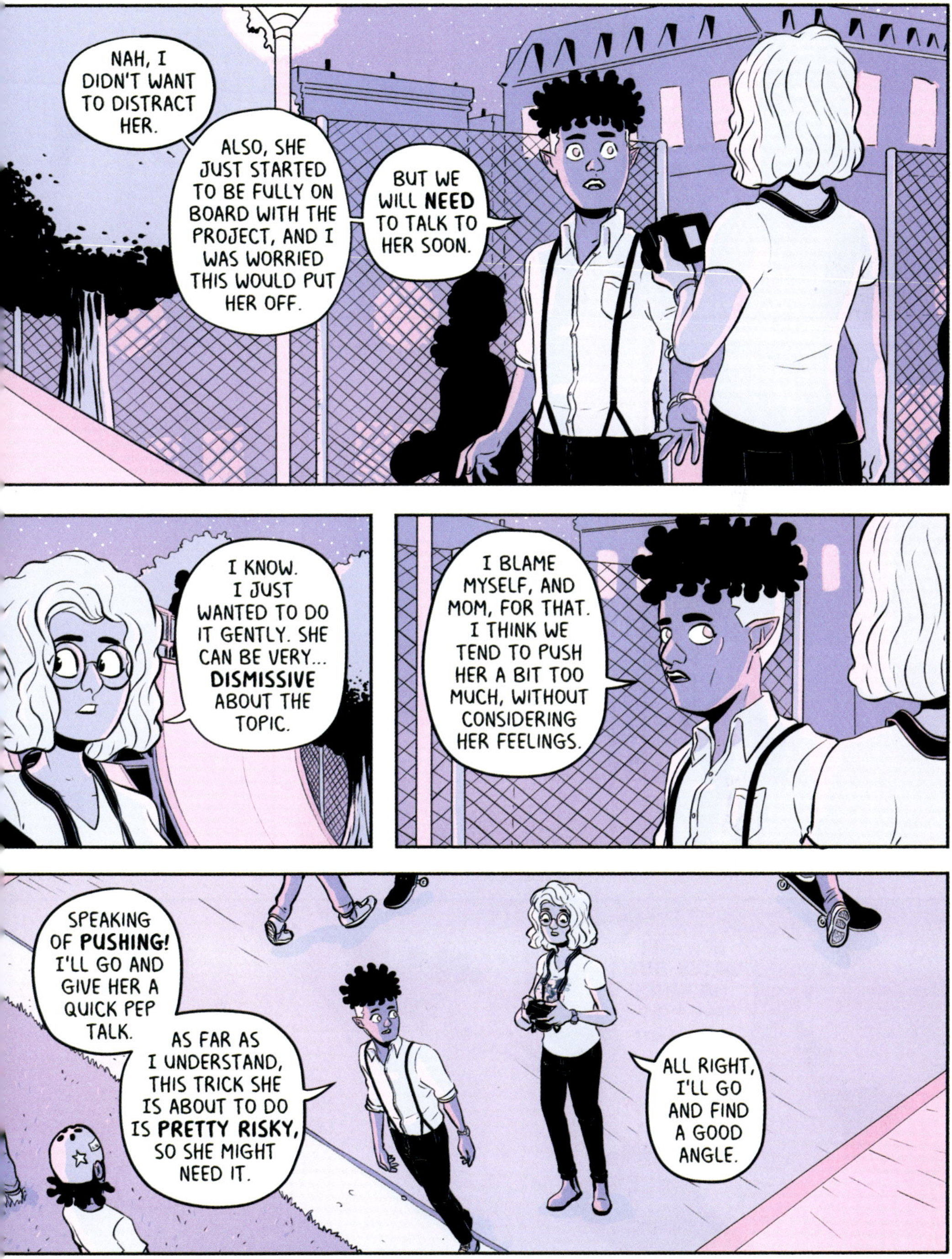

NAH, I DIDN'T WANT TO DISTRACT HER.
ALSO, SHE JUST STARTED TO BE FULLY ON BOARD WITH THE PROJECT, AND I WAS WORRIED THIS WOULD PUT HER OFF.
BUT WE WILL **NEED** TO TALK TO HER SOON.

HEY, PEPPS

WOULD YOU GIVE US A HAND? THIS THING IS VERY SL--

THWAPP!

SLIDE

HEY, JEB! **WATCH OUT!** THE RAMPS ARE A BIT **SLIPPERY!**
MRRFF DNFF...
ALSO DON'T CALL ME *PEPPS!*
WHAT?

I WAS JUST COMING HERE TO GIVE YOU SOME **ENCOURAGEMENT!**
I WAS TRYING TO BE **NICE!**
ALL RIGHT, ALL RIGHT! HOPE YOU DIDN'T HURT YOURSELF!

I HEAL FAST. MAINLY 'CAUSE I DRINK MY B+ JUICE! UNLIKE YOU!
HAVE YOU HAD ANY TODAY?

I HAVE IT HERE WITH ME! DON'T YOU WORRY!

ONE OF US HAS TO. JUST GIVE US A SHOUT WHEN YOU ARE READY.

YOU GOT YOUR **BAT SPINACH** READY, POPEYE?

WHAT?

I WAS JUST JOKING! SEE YOU AT THE PIZZA PARTY, PEPPER!
WOOMM...

BAT SPINACH, MY BUTT!

ALL RIGHT, LET DO THIS!

WHOOOSHH...

FWWHHHA

WH

POP!
FLIP!
KRACK!

THUDD!

PEPPER!
SOMEONE CALL AN AMBULANCE!
IS SHE ALIVE?
SHE IS A **VAMPIRE**, YOU DINGUS!
DO AMBULANCES EVEN TREAT VAMPIRES?
NO NEED TO WORRY ABOUT THAT. SHE SHOULD BE FINE IN A MINUTE, RIGHT, PEPPS?
PEPPER, **SAY SOMETHING!**
GRAVE GRIND
NNNNNGH...

PEPPER, DID YOU DRINK YOUR B+ JUICE?
HNNN...
GREAT...

SORRY, GUYS, WE HAVE TO POSTPONE THE PIZZA PARTY.
ALSO, I NEED A COUPLE OF YOU TO HELP HAUL PEPPER INTO MY CAR.
I'LL DO IT!

JEB?
DON'T WORRY, ANA. SHE WILL BE RIGHT AS RAIN. SHE JUST NEEDS TO BE FED.

SPEAR MINT CONDITION
ANTIQUE & SECOND

ANTIQUE BOOKS
CLOSED

ANA.

NNH...YEAH, 'M AWAKE!
OH MY. YOU JUST PASSED OUT.
STRESS WILL DO THAT TO YOU. YOU MUST HAVE BEEN **REALLY** WORRIED.

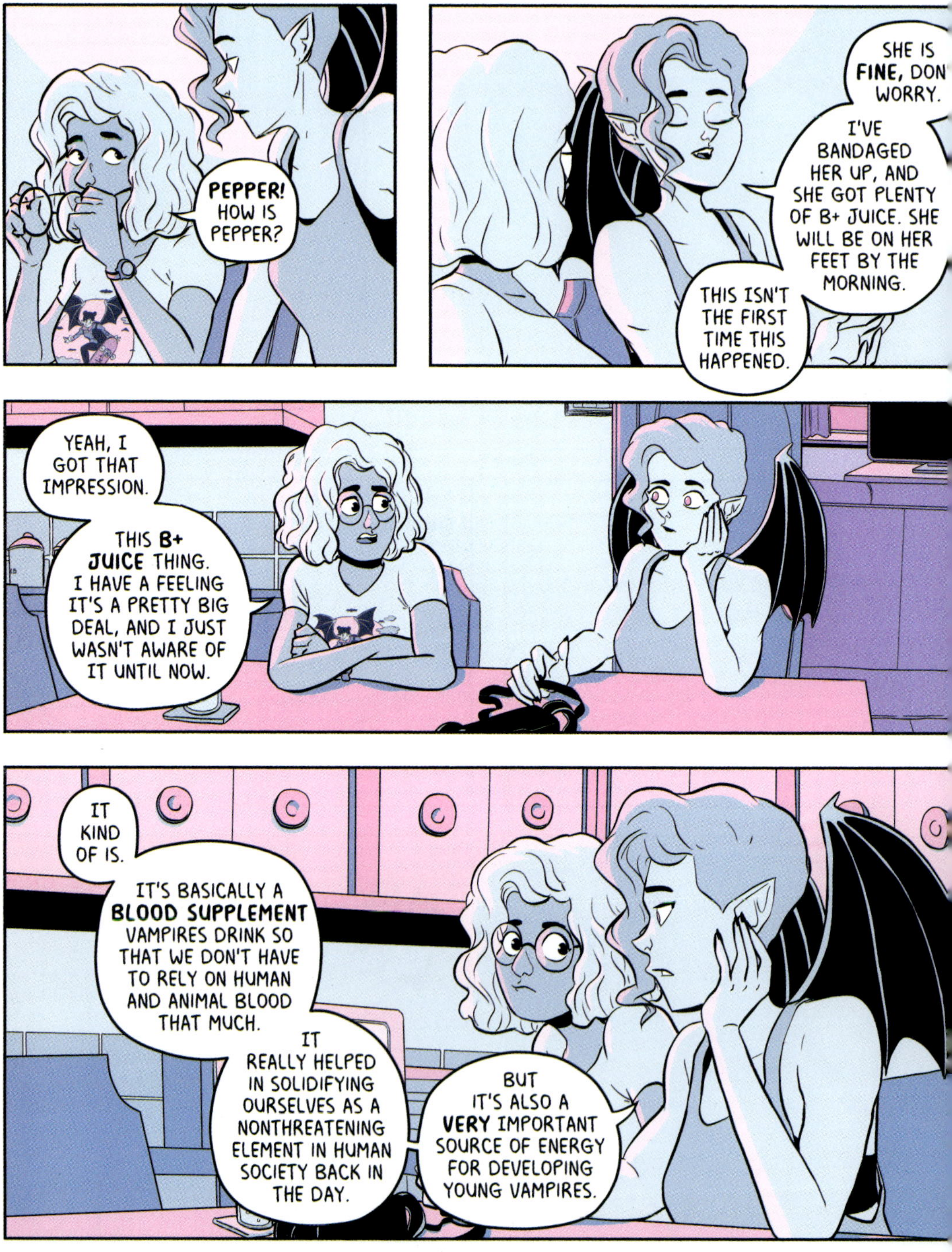

IT KIND OF IS.

IT'S BASICALLY A **BLOOD SUPPLEMENT** VAMPIRES DRINK SO THAT WE DON'T HAVE TO RELY ON HUMAN AND ANIMAL BLOOD THAT MUCH.

IT REALLY HELPED IN SOLIDIFYING OURSELVES AS A NONTHREATENING ELEMENT IN HUMAN SOCIETY BACK IN THE DAY.

BUT IT'S ALSO A **VERY** IMPORTANT SOURCE OF ENERGY FOR DEVELOPING YOUNG VAMPIRES.

AND PEPPER IS SKIPPING OUT ON IT.
SHE IS DRINKING IT, BUT JUST THE **BARE MINIMUM.**
I SUSPECT IT'S RELATED TO SKATEBOARDING SOMEHOW.

SO IS THAT WHY SHE WASN'T HEALING FASTER?
YES. SHE LIVES A FAIRLY ACTIVE LIFESTYLE, WHILE IGNORING THAT HER BODY IS PREPARING ITSELF FOR **IMMORTALITY.** SHE **NEEDS** SLEEP AND SHE **NEEDS** THE B+ JUICE, BUT SHE REGULARLY SKIPS OUT ON BOTH.

LIKE THE FIRST TIME YOU MET HER, WHEN YOU HAD TO CARRY HER HOME.
IT'S **NOT** A NEW THING.
SIGH!

HEY, PEPPER. HOW YOU DOING?
KNOCK KNOCK

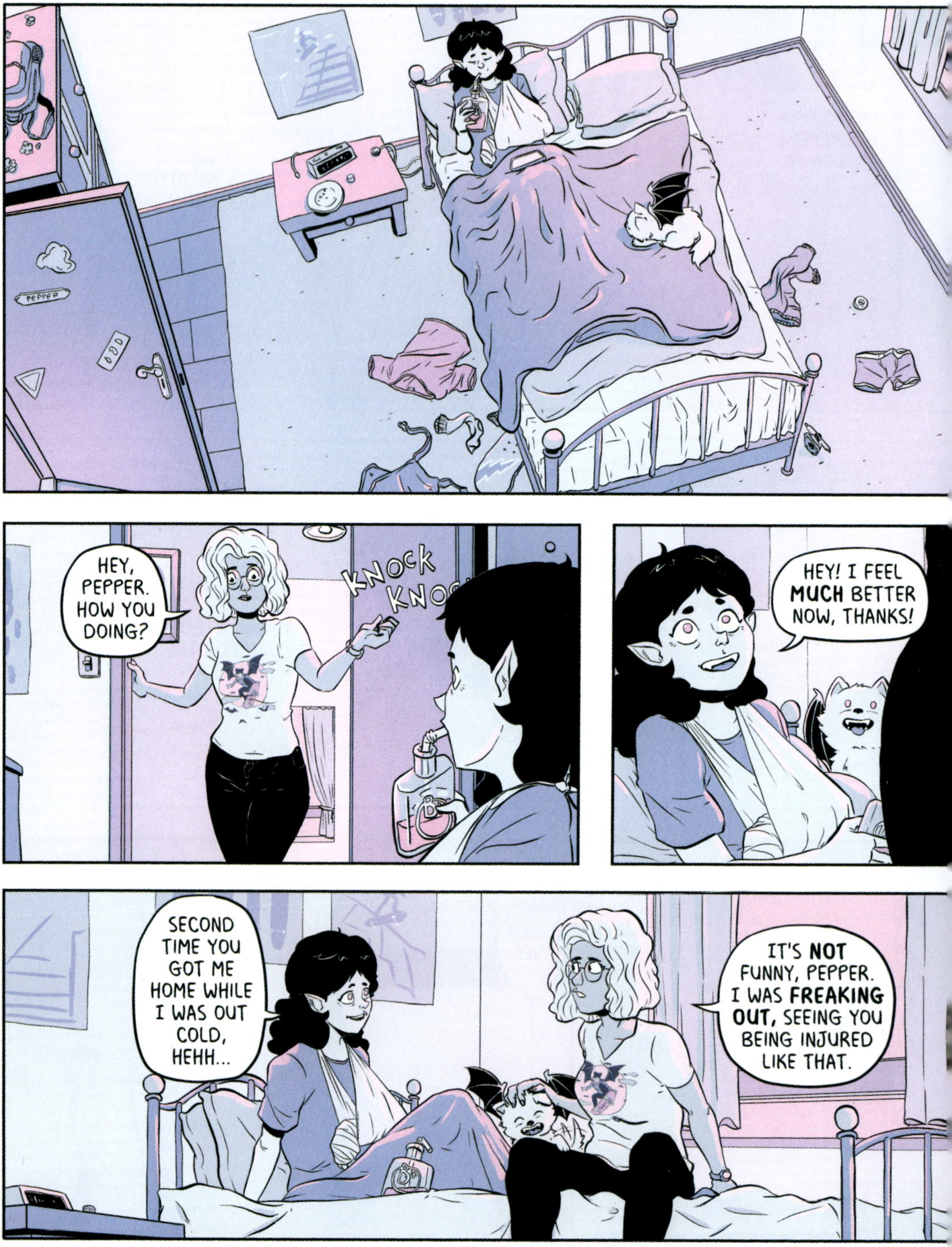

HEY! I FEEL **MUCH** BETTER NOW, THANKS!

SECOND TIME YOU GOT ME HOME WHILE I WAS OUT COLD, HEHH...
IT'S **NOT** FUNNY, PEPPER. I WAS **FREAKING OUT,** SEEING YOU BEING INJURED LIKE THAT.

YOU ARE RIGHT. I'M NOT IN THE MOOD TO JOKE EITHER.
BUT I BOUNCED BACK, SO IT'S ALL GOOD. I **ALWAYS** BOUNCE BACK.

THAT'S THE PROBLEM, THOUGH! YOU **DIDN'T!** YOU DIDN'T BOUNCE BACK!

AND I KNOW IT'S BECAUSE YOU DON'T DRINK ENOUGH **B+ JUICE!** YOUR MOM AND JEB TOLD ME.

TYPICAL... THEY ARE **ALWAYS** INTERFERING.

WELL, SOMEONE **HAD TO,** BECAUSE **YOU** DIDN'T TELL ME!
'CAUSE IT'S A **PRIVATE THING!**
NO IT'S **NOT!** NOT IF WE HAVE TO SCRAPE YOU OFF THE GROUND AND DRAG YOUR LIMP BODY HOME BECAUSE YOU **REFUSE** TO DRINK IT!
I WAS **VERY** SCARED, PEPPER!
THIS WAS THE SECOND TIME YOU SCARED ME LIKE THAT!

OKAY, IT WON'T HAPPEN AGAIN.

BECAUSE YOU **WILL** BE DRINKING YOUR JUICE LIKE YOU'RE **SUPPOSED** TO?

RIGHT

SHRUG...

PEPPER, WHY ARE YOU DOING THIS? TALK TO ME, PLEASE!

YOU **KNOW** WHY!

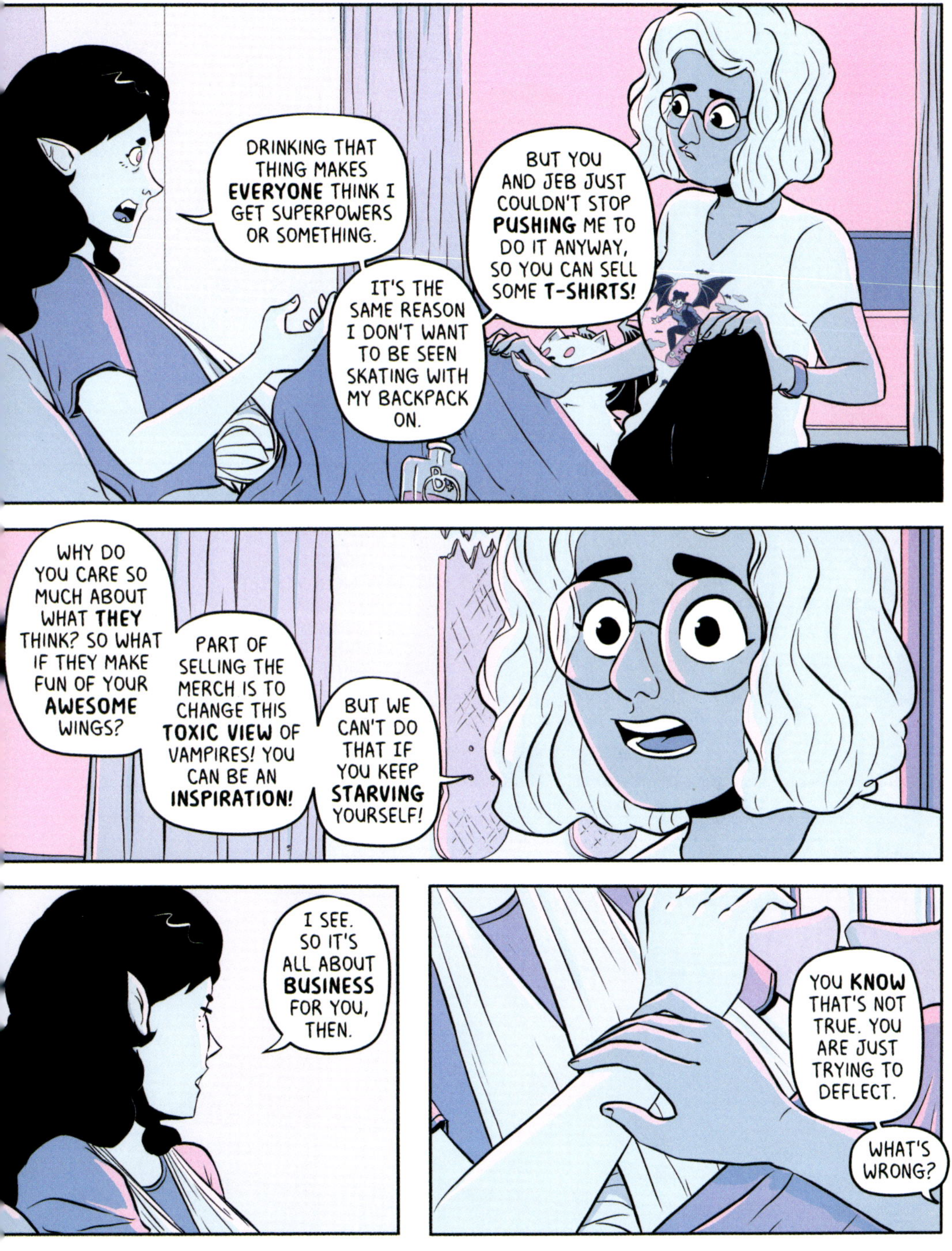

DRINKING THAT THING MAKES **EVERYONE** THINK I GET SUPERPOWERS OR SOMETHING.
IT'S THE SAME REASON I DON'T WANT TO BE SEEN SKATING WITH MY BACKPACK ON.
BUT YOU AND JEB JUST COULDN'T STOP **PUSHING** ME TO DO IT ANYWAY, SO YOU CAN SELL SOME **T-SHIRTS!**

WHAT'S **WRONG** IS THAT YOU AND MY BROTHER ARE HIDING SOMETHING!
WHAT?

I **HEARD** YOU! IN THE PARK, BEFORE I TRIED TO DO THE TRICK. I HAVE **VERY** GOOD EARS, ANA!
I **KNOW** YOU AND JEB ARE KEEPING SOMETHING FROM ME!
WE WANTED TO TELL YOU, BUT ONLY AFTER THE SHOOT! I KNEW IT WOULD UPSET YOU, AND I WAS AFRAID YOU WOULD BE TOO DISTRACTED!

WELL, YOU WERE RIGHT! I **AM** UPSET!
SO, WHAT IS IT?

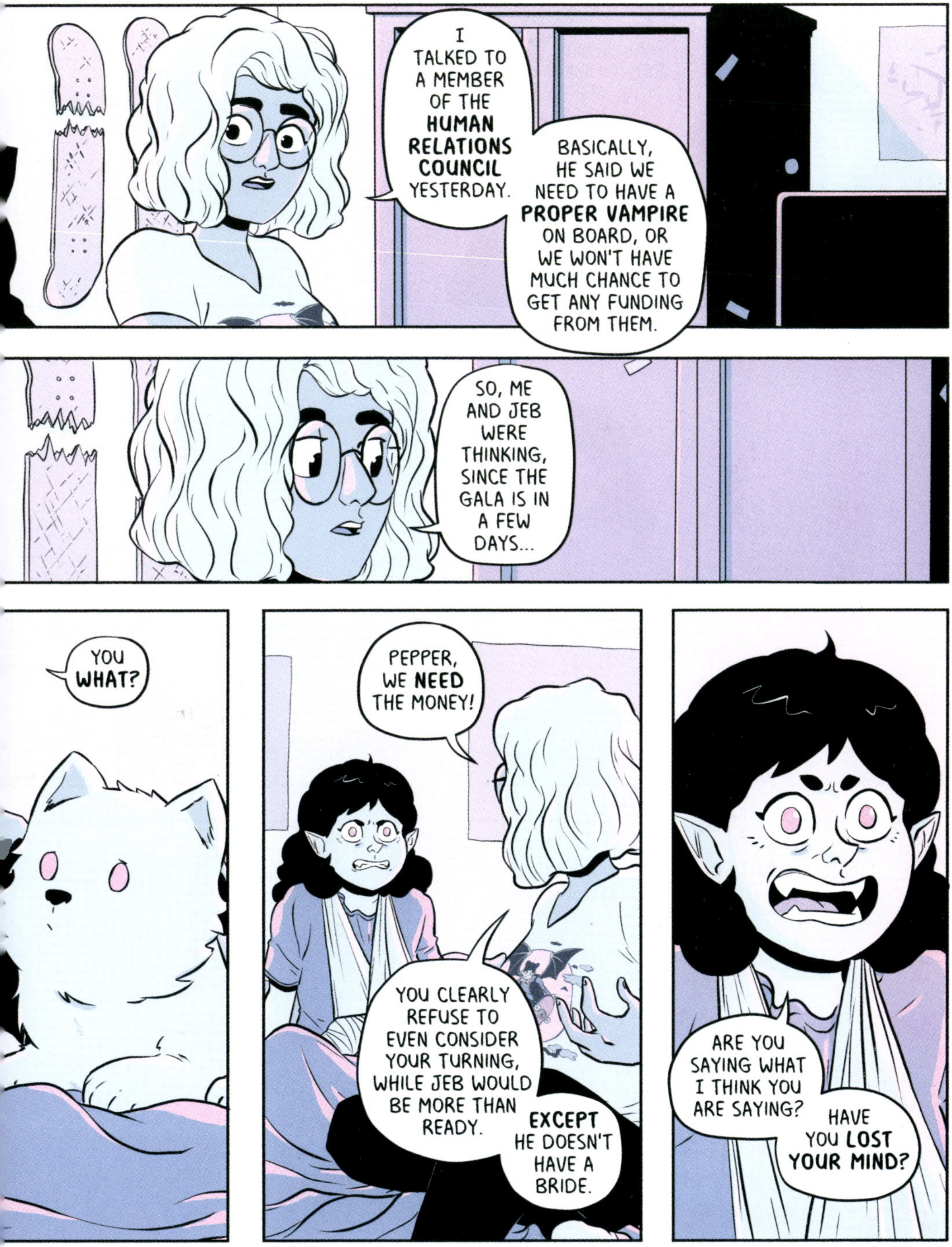

I TALKED TO A MEMBER OF THE HUMAN RELATIONS COUNCIL YESTERDAY.
BASICALLY, HE SAID WE NEED TO HAVE A PROPER VAMPIRE ON BOARD, OR WE WON'T HAVE MUCH CHANCE TO GET ANY FUNDING FROM THEM.

SO, ME AND JEB WERE THINKING, SINCE THE GALA IS IN A FEW DAYS...

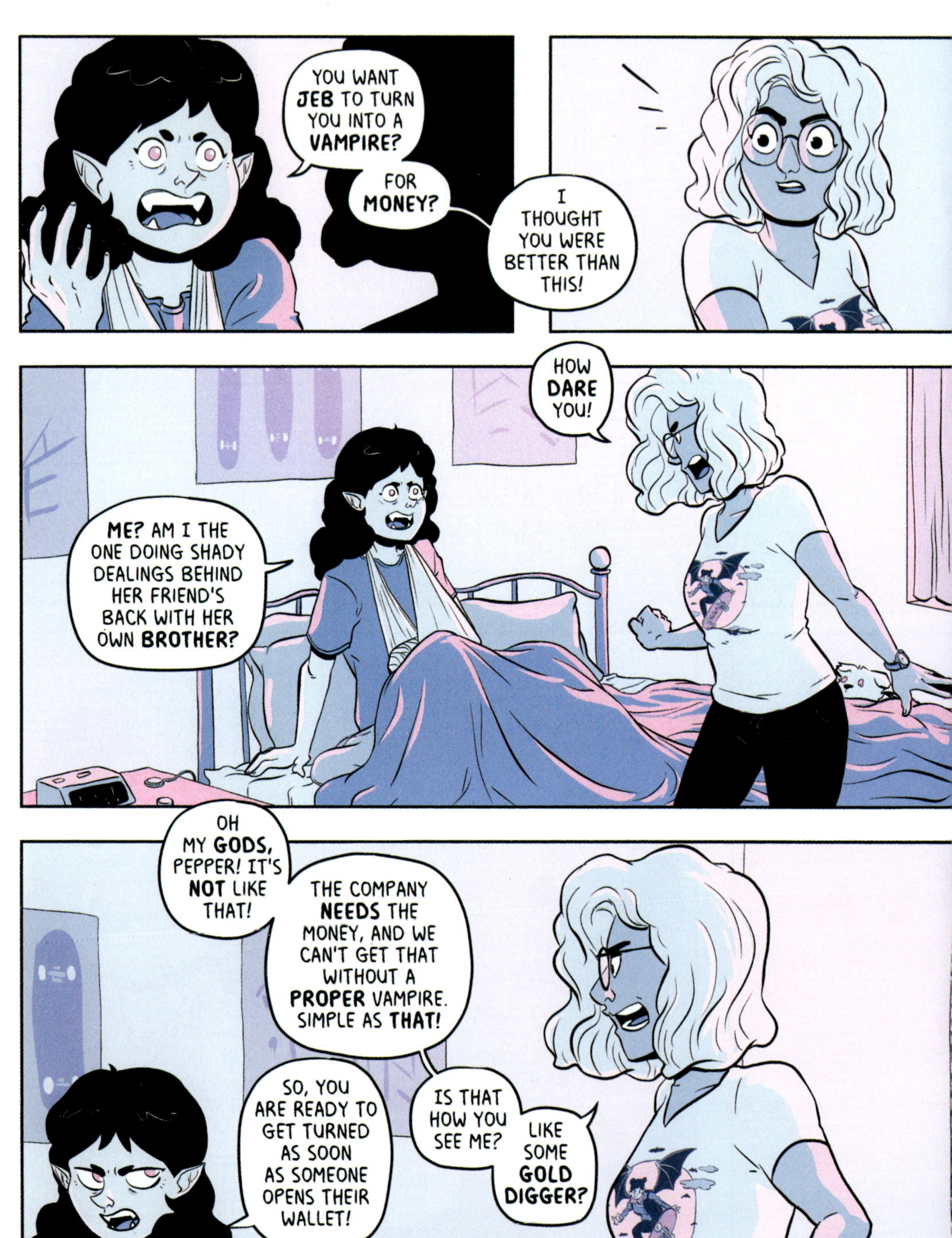
YOU WANT JEB TO TURN YOU INTO A VAMPIRE?
FOR MONEY?
I THOUGHT YOU WERE BETTER THAN THIS!
HOW DARE YOU!
ME? AM I THE ONE DOING SHADY DEALINGS BEHIND HER FRIEND'S BACK WITH HER OWN BROTHER?
OH MY GODS, PEPPER! IT'S NOT LIKE THAT!
THE COMPANY NEEDS THE MONEY, AND WE CAN'T GET THAT WITHOUT A PROPER VAMPIRE. SIMPLE AS THAT!
SO, YOU ARE READY TO GET TURNED AS SOON AS SOMEONE OPENS THEIR WALLET!
IS THAT HOW YOU SEE ME?
LIKE SOME GOLD DIGGER?

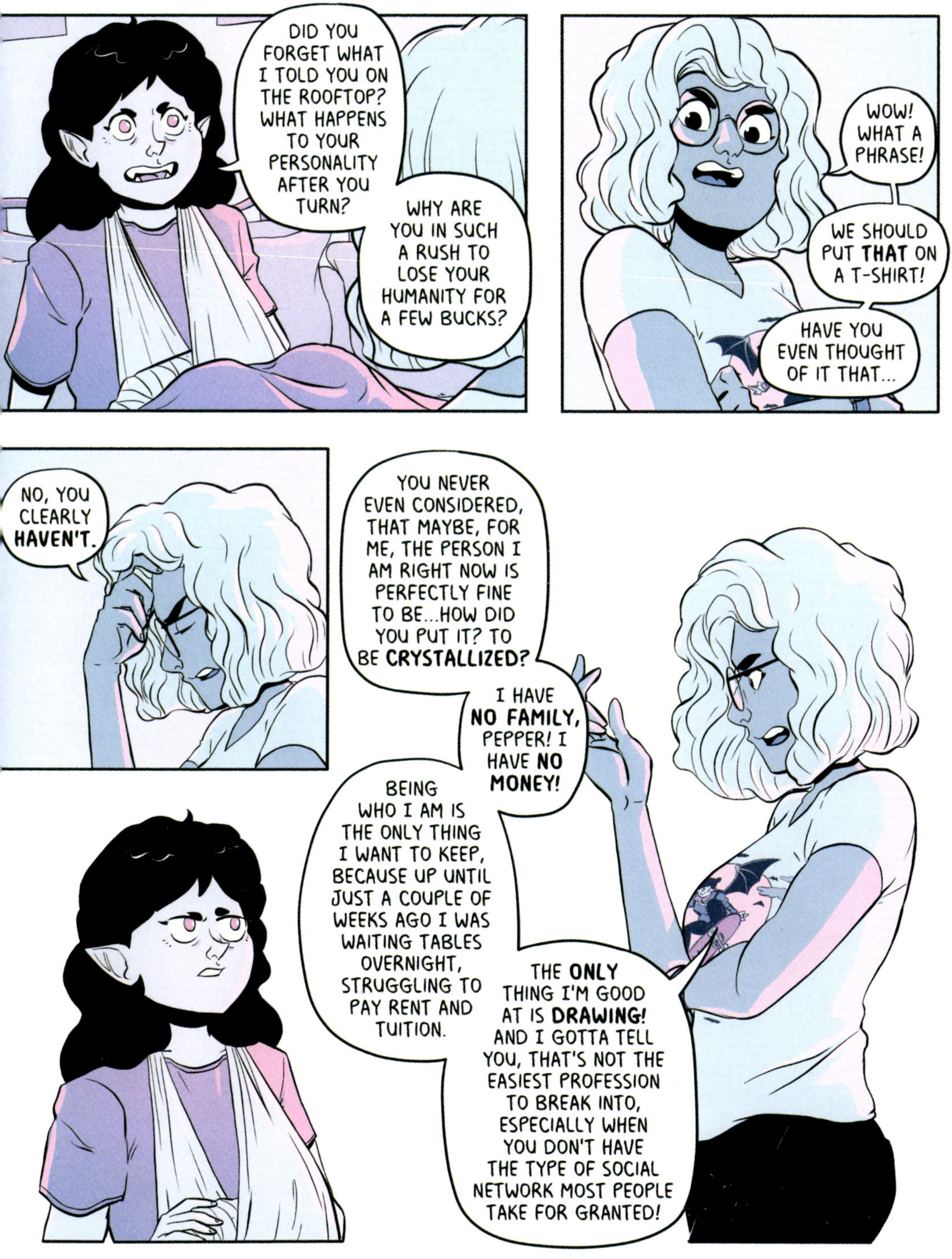

NO, YOU CLEARLY **HAVEN'T**.

YOU NEVER EVEN CONSIDERED, THAT MAYBE, FOR ME, THE PERSON I AM RIGHT NOW IS PERFECTLY FINE TO BE...HOW DID YOU PUT IT? TO BE **CRYSTALLIZED?**

I HAVE **NO FAMILY,** PEPPER! I HAVE **NO MONEY!**

BEING WHO I AM IS THE ONLY THING I WANT TO KEEP, BECAUSE UP UNTIL JUST A COUPLE OF WEEKS AGO I WAS WAITING TABLES OVERNIGHT, STRUGGLING TO PAY RENT AND TUITION.

THE **ONLY** THING I'M GOOD AT IS **DRAWING!** AND I GOTTA TELL YOU, THAT'S NOT THE EASIEST PROFESSION TO BREAK INTO, ESPECIALLY WHEN YOU DON'T HAVE THE TYPE OF SOCIAL NETWORK MOST PEOPLE TAKE FOR GRANTED!

I USED TO HAVE **NOTHING,** AND JUST A FEW WEEKS AFTER I MET YOU AND YOUR FAMILY, I SUDDENLY HAVE A FUTURE TO LOOK FORWARD TO.
YOU SAY I WOULD SACRIFICE MY HUMANITY FOR MONEY.
I SAY I WOULD THROW MY USELESS PAST IN THE TRASH IN A **HEARTBEAT** FOR THE PROMISE OF AN EVERLASTING LIFE THAT COMES WITH AN INSTANT FAMILY, COMMUNITY, AND PURPOSE.

IT'S LITERALLY **EVERYTHING** I NEVER HAD BUT ALWAYS WANTED! BUT INSTEAD OF **HELPING ME,** YOU JUST ACT LIKE A **SPOILED BRAT!**
OH, LOOK AT MISS **HIGH AND MIGHTY!** DEMANDING TO BE **TURNED** INTO VAMPIRE AND...

WAIT!

HELPING YOU? YOU WANT ME TO HELP **YOU**...TO TURN?
IS THAT WHAT YOU WERE PLANNING **ALL ALONG?** IS THAT WHY MOM HIRED YOU?
PEPPER... NO...

EVEN IF YOU DIDN'T DELIBERATELY SIGN UP TO BE TURNED, I BET A PRETTY PENNY YOU **WERE** ANGLING FOR IT!
PEPPER, YOU ARE MAKING THINGS UP!

AM I? DID I MAKE UP THAT MY MOM HIRED THE **ONLY** PERSON I'VE SHOWN **ANY** INTEREST IN?

DID I MAKE UP JEB WORMING HIS WAY INTO THE **ONLY** THING THAT MAKES ME HAPPY?
DID I MAKE UP MOM JUST CASUALLY TOSSING US IN FRONT OF THE VAMPIRE COUNCIL?

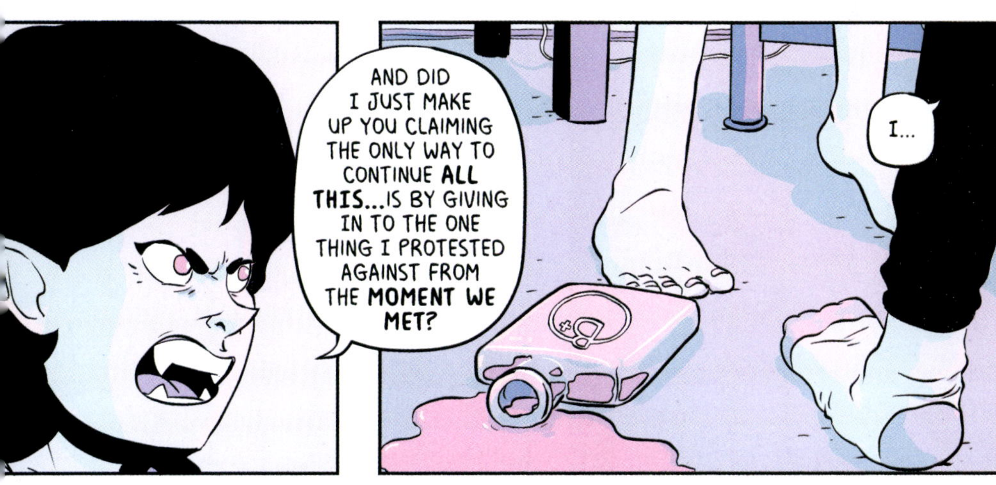
AND DID I JUST MAKE UP YOU CLAIMING THE ONLY WAY TO CONTINUE **ALL THIS...** IS BY GIVING IN TO THE ONE THING I PROTESTED AGAINST FROM THE **MOMENT WE MET?**
I...

GET OUT OF MY ROOM.

PEPPER, YOU DON--

NOW!

03
MINT

1338 BOI

SO...

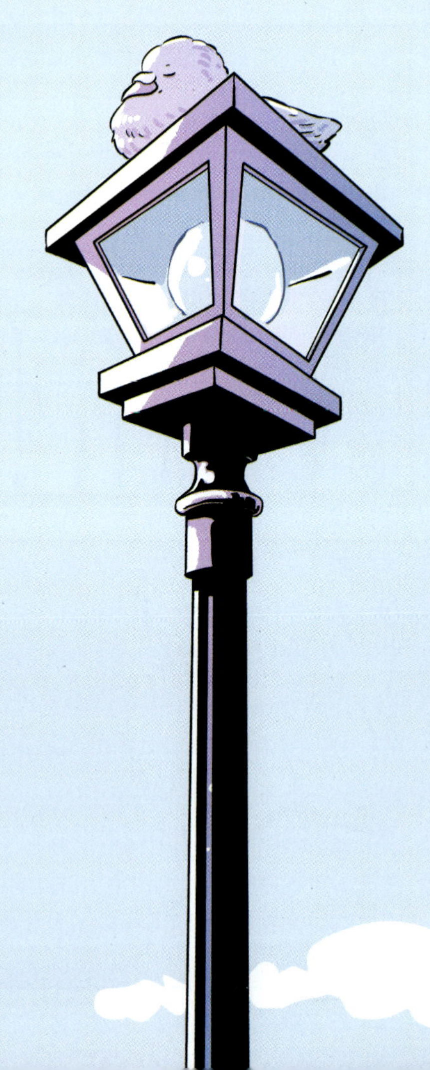

TAP
TAP
TAP
TAP
TAP
TAP

TAP
TAP
TAP

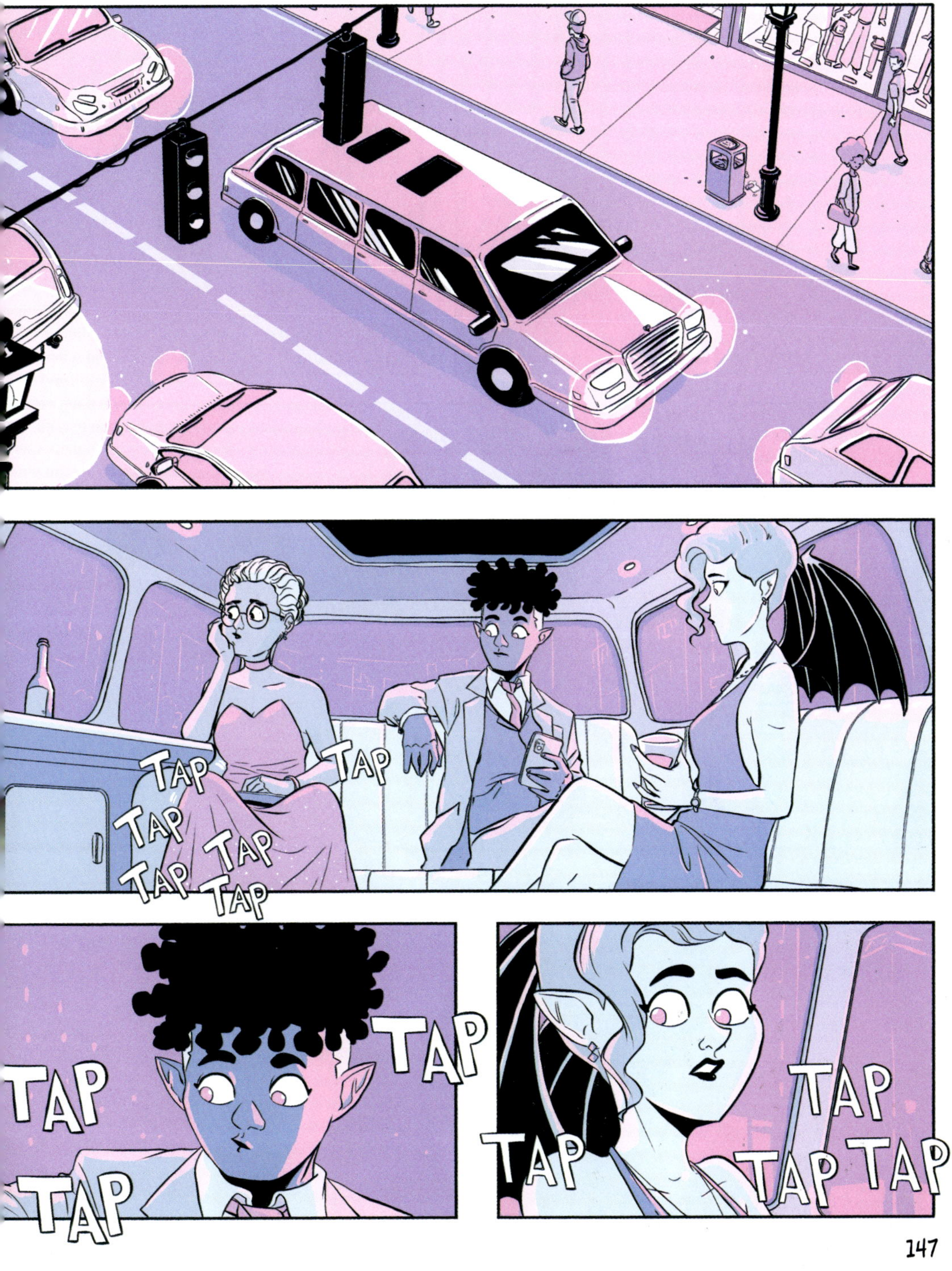

TAP
TAP
TAP
TAP

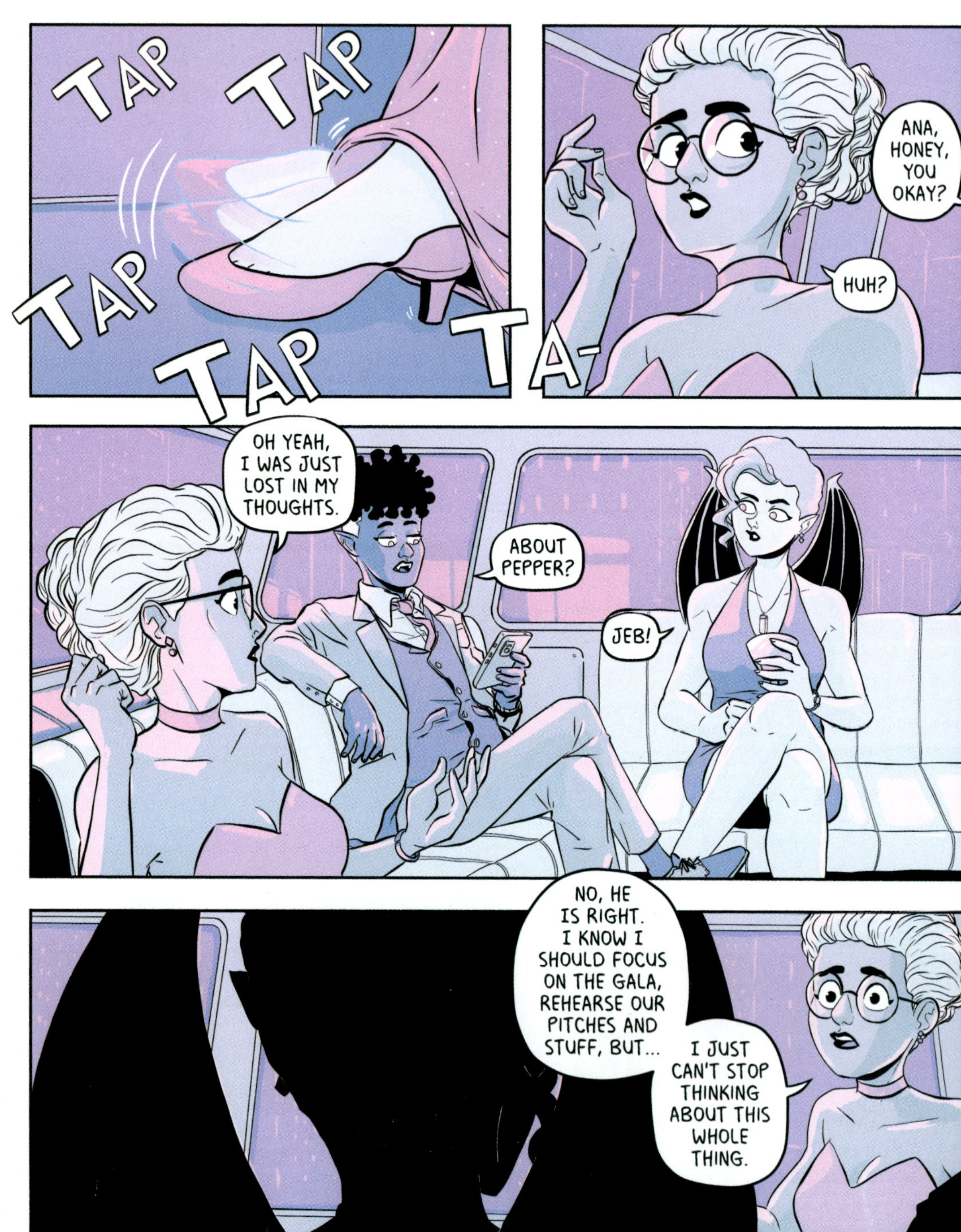
TAP TAP
TAP
TAP TA-
ANA, HONEY, YOU OKAY?
HUH?
OH YEAH, I WAS JUST LOST IN MY THOUGHTS.
ABOUT PEPPER?
JEB!
NO, HE IS RIGHT. I KNOW I SHOULD FOCUS ON THE GALA, REHEARSE OUR PITCHES AND STUFF, BUT...
I JUST CAN'T STOP THINKING ABOUT THIS WHOLE THING.

SHE REFUSED TO TALK TO ME, DIDN'T ANSWER MY TEXTS EITHER.
I KNOW SHE IS BEING STUBBORN, BUT I STILL FEEL AWFUL ABOUT IT.

SIGH...

YOU TRIED, HONEY. NOTHING MORE YOU CAN DO. PEPPER IS JUST BEING PEPPER. BUT **SHE'LL BE** AT THE GALA. YOU'LL SEE.

I WOULDN'T WORRY ABOUT OUR PITCH, EITHER. THE VIDEOS ARE GOING STRONG ON ALL OUR SOCIALS, AND I GOT **FIVE** DIFFERENT PRODUCT ROLL-OUT PLANS LINED UP ALREADY IN A PDF THAT I CAN PULL UP ON MY PHONE IF I HAVE TO.
STILL...

ALSO I SNUCK INTO HER ROOM WHILE SHE WAS SHOWERING, AND LEFT HER NEW SUIT AND THE INVITATION ON HER BED. IN CASE SHE CHANGES HER MIND.
MOM...

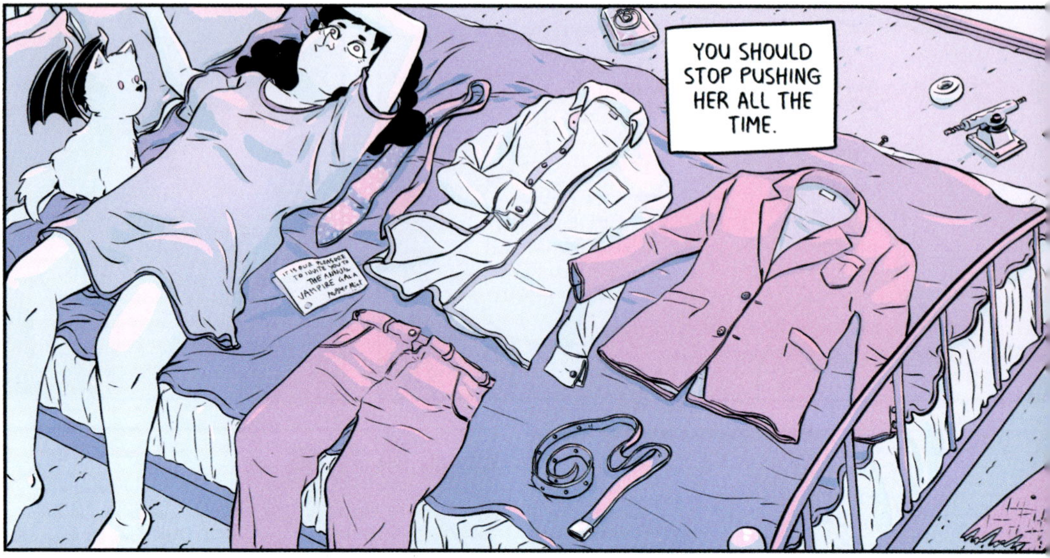

YOU SHOULD STOP PUSHING HER ALL THE TIME.

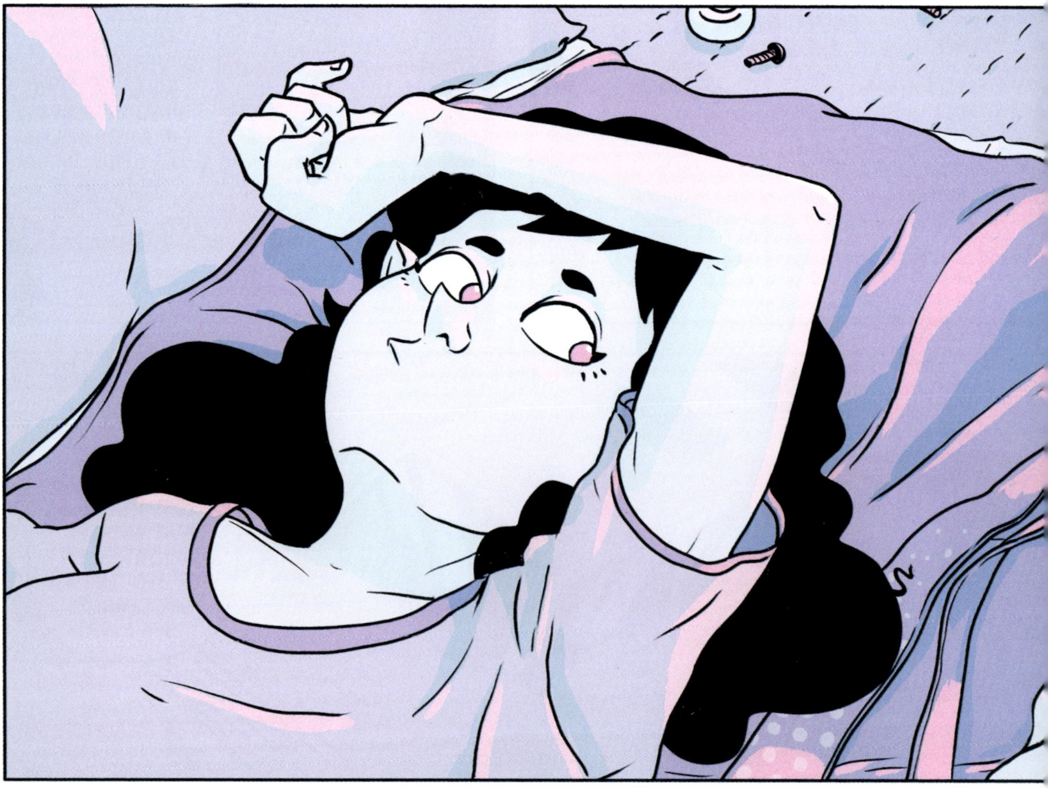

WELCOME TO THE ANNUAL VAMPIRE GALA

I SEE...
THAT'S QUITE A PITCH, MR. MINT AND MISS WHYTE.
TOLD YOU THEY HAVE POTENTIAL.
THANKS, MR. PEAS.
YES, BUT I THOUGHT THERE WAS SUPPOSED TO BE A **THIRD** PERSON IN THIS COMPANY. MR. MINT'S SISTER, PEPPER?
I WAS UNDER THE IMPRESSIO HER **TURNIN** WILL BE ON OF THE ANNOUNCEMEN TONIGHT.

PEPPER WASN'T FEELING TOO WELL, SO SHE DECIDED IT'S BEST TO SKIP THE GALA THIS TIME.
BUT HER ANNOUNCEMENT WOULDN'T HAVE BEEN THE ONE HAPPENING TODAY ANYWAY.
RIGHT, ANA?

UMM, YES, YES. QUITE RIGHT.
CALLING **ALL** ATTENDEES! THE ANNOUNCEMENTS WILL TAKE PLACE IN A FEW MINUTES!
PLEASE TAKE YOUR SEATS. AND WILL ALL THE GROOMS AND BRIDES GATHER AT THE BACK OF THE STAGE?

SORRY, BUT WE GOTTA DASH!
MAKE SURE TO CALL MY OFFICE ON MONDAY IF WE DON'T HAVE THE CHANCE TO CATCH UP LATER!

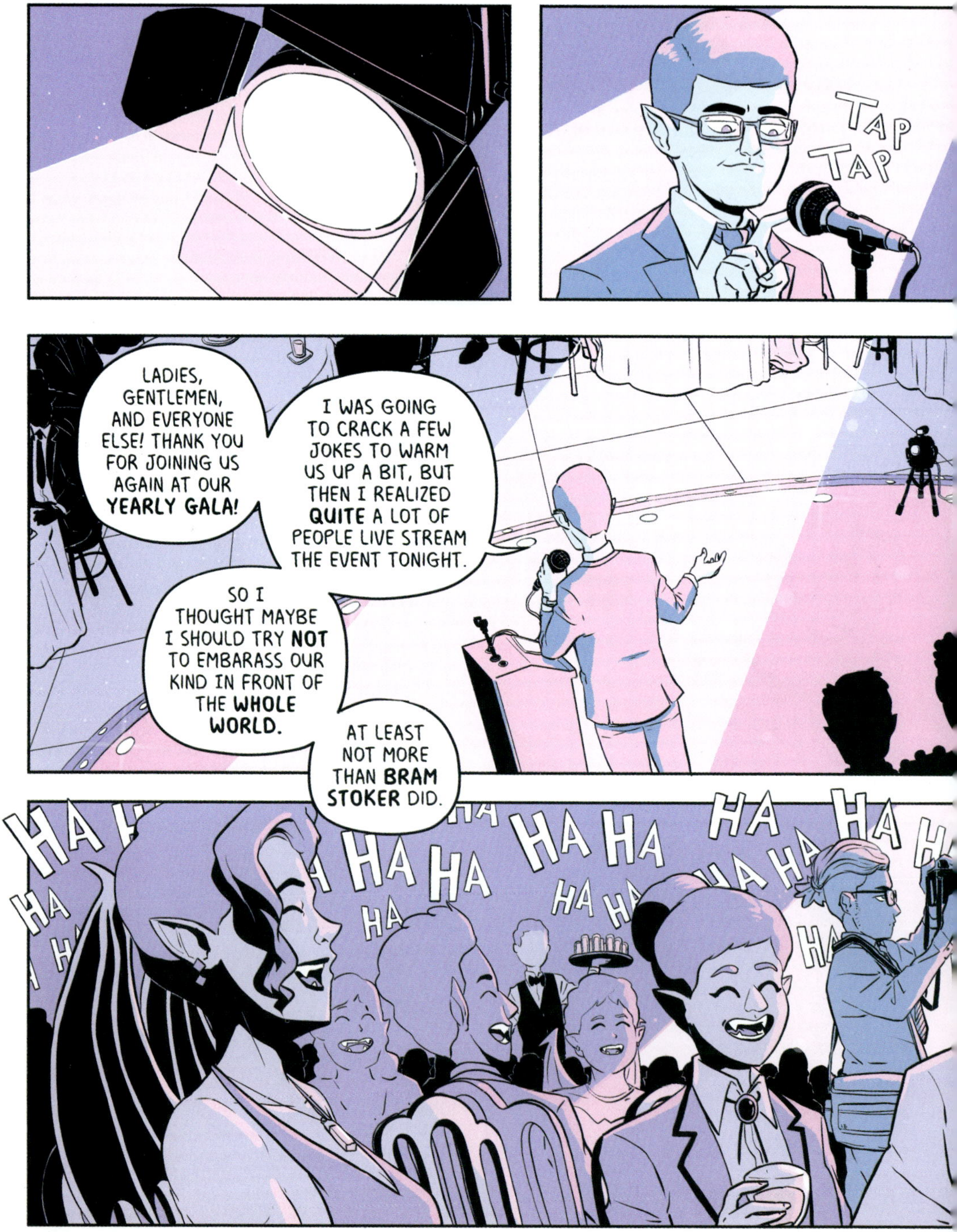

LADIES, GENTLEMEN, AND EVERYONE ELSE! THANK YOU FOR JOINING US AGAIN AT OUR **YEARLY GALA!**

I WAS GOING TO CRACK A FEW JOKES TO WARM US UP A BIT, BUT THEN I REALIZED **QUITE** A LOT OF PEOPLE LIVE STREAM THE EVENT TONIGHT.

SO I THOUGHT MAYBE I SHOULD TRY **NOT** TO EMBARASS OUR KIND IN FRONT OF THE **WHOLE WORLD.**

AT LEAST NOT MORE THAN **BRAM STOKER** DID.

HA HA HA HA HA HA

SWIFTLY MOVING ON, OW THAT I'VE **UNLEASHED** HE WRATH OF UNDREDS OF LITERARY SCHOLARS...
TO THE **HIGHLIGHT** OF OUR EVENING, WHEN I GET TO ANNOUNCE THIS YEAR'S SOON-TO-BE-TURNED **BRIDES** AND THEIR **GROOMS!**

SO, WITHOUT FURTHER ADO...

CLAP
CLAP
CLAP
CLAP
CLAP
CLAP
RESERVED FOR:
PEPPER MINT
CLAP

RESERVED FOR:
PEPPER MINT

HEY! WE ARE COMING UP!

BELIEVE IT OR NOT, I WISH PEPPER WAS HERE TOO, BUT I NEED YOU TO PUT A SMILE ON YOUR FACE NOW...

bite
skate with a bloodlust!
GRAVE GRIND
COFFIN FLIP
MOM IS RIGHT. PEPPER WILL COME AROUND EVENTUALLY.

CLICK!

LET'S GO, SHROOM!

MOM, JEB, ANA,
HOPE THE GALA WAS
FUN AND THE TURNING
WENT WELL.
I DECIDED I CAN'T BE
A PART OF THIS ANYMORE.
SO I LEFT.
I HAVE SHROOM AND MY
SAVINGS, SO I'LL BE JUST
FINE.

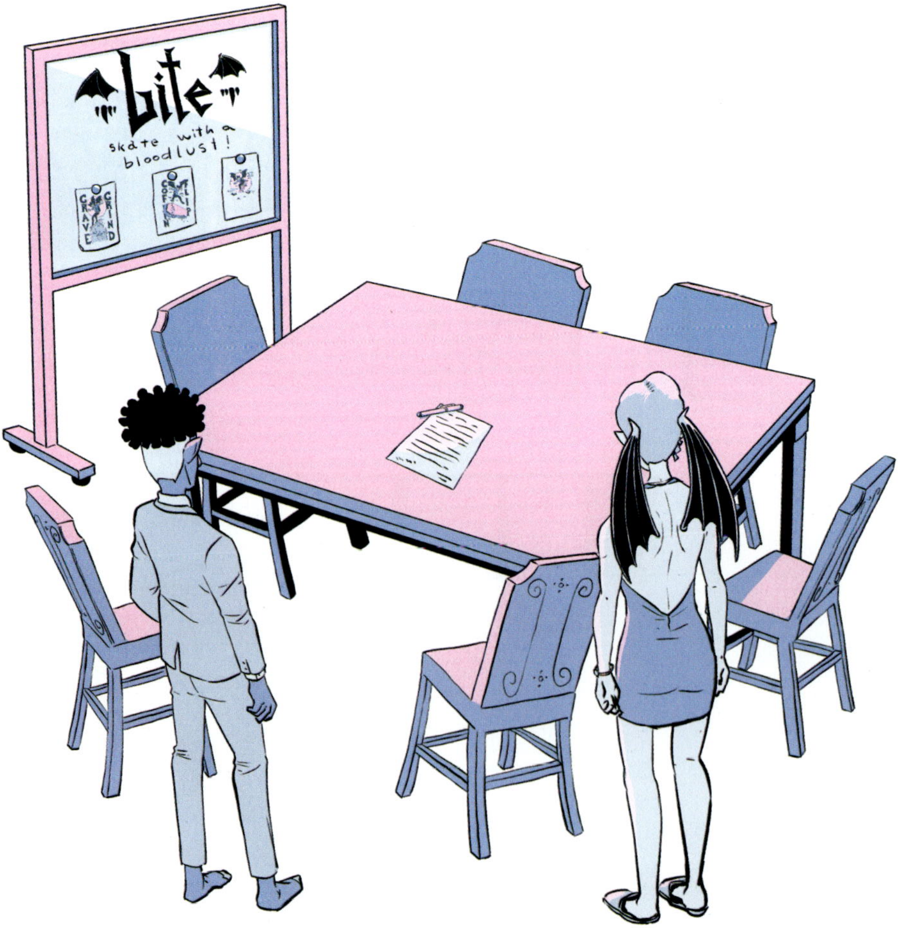

bite
skate with a bloodlust!

MOM, JEB, ANA,
HOPE THE GALA WAS FUN AND THE TURNING WENT WELL.
I DECIDED I CAN'T BE A PART OF THIS ANYMORE, SO I LEFT.
I HAVE SHROOM AND MY SAVINGS, SO I'LL BE JUST FINE.
P.S. DON'T TRY TO FIND ME!
PEPPER
+SHROOM

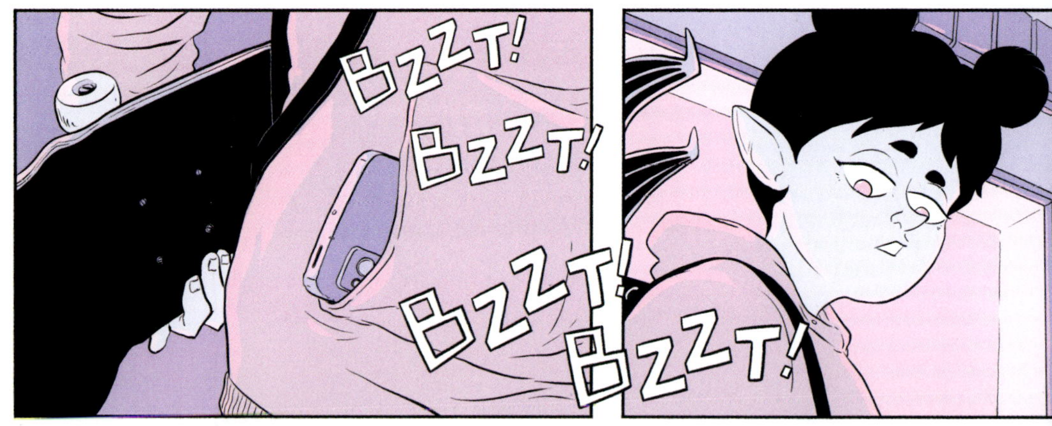
BZZT!
BZZT!
BZZT!
BZZT!

JUST A SECOND, SHROOM.
MMRR?

10:14
FRIDAY, 17 JUNE
NEW MESSAGE
NEW VOICE MESSAGE
NEW VOICE MESSAGE
VOICE MESS...
VOICE MESS...
CE MESS

NEW MESSAGE
NEW VOICE MESSAGE
NEW VOICE MESSAGE FROM MOM
EW VOICE MESSA
VOICE MESS

MUT
ELETE

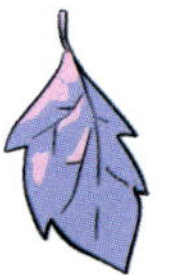

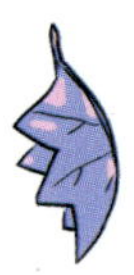

MONTHS
PASS...

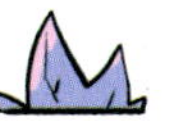

BEEP
BEEP

BEEP
4:30
SNOOZE
BEEP
Bzzt!

Bzzt!
4:30
BEEP
BEEP

BEEP
BEEP
BEEP
NNHH...

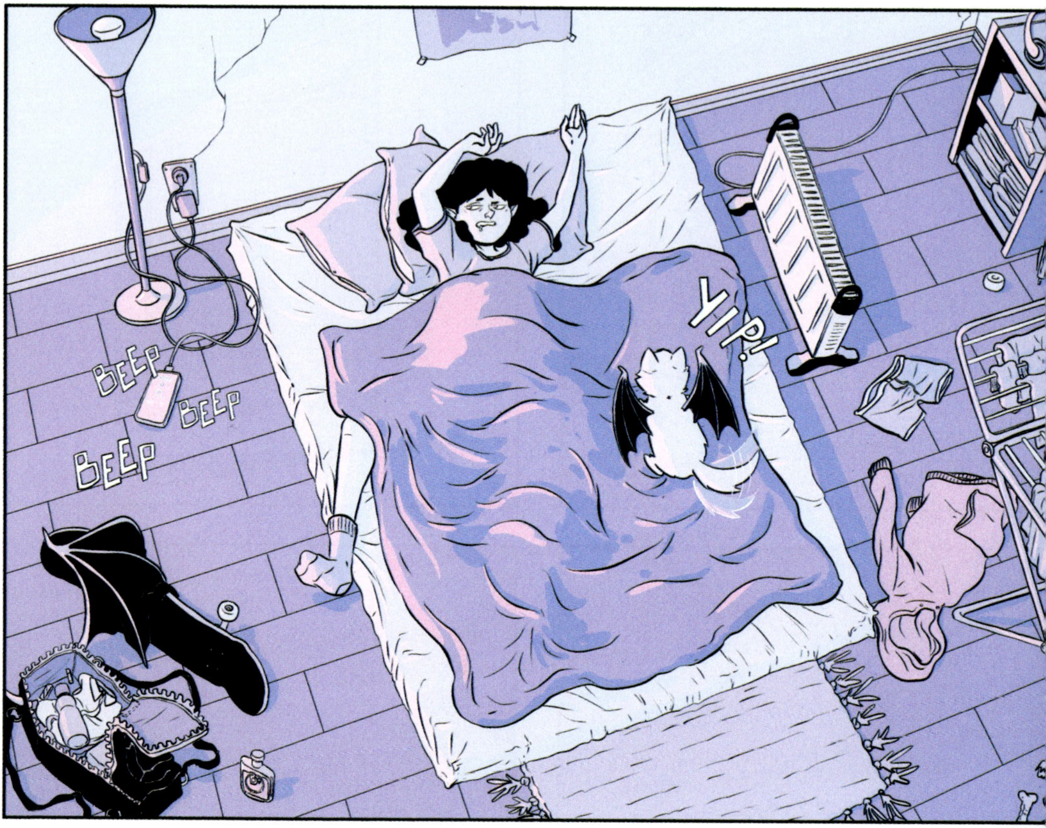

YIP!
BEEP
BEEP
BEEP

SKIFF
SKIFF
SKIFF

SKIFF
SKIFF

SO, WE HAVE STIR-FRY NOODLES WITH A DASH OF B+ JUICE, OR MICROWAVE RICE.
GOLDEN VEGETABLE RICE
YIP!
GOOD CHOICE!

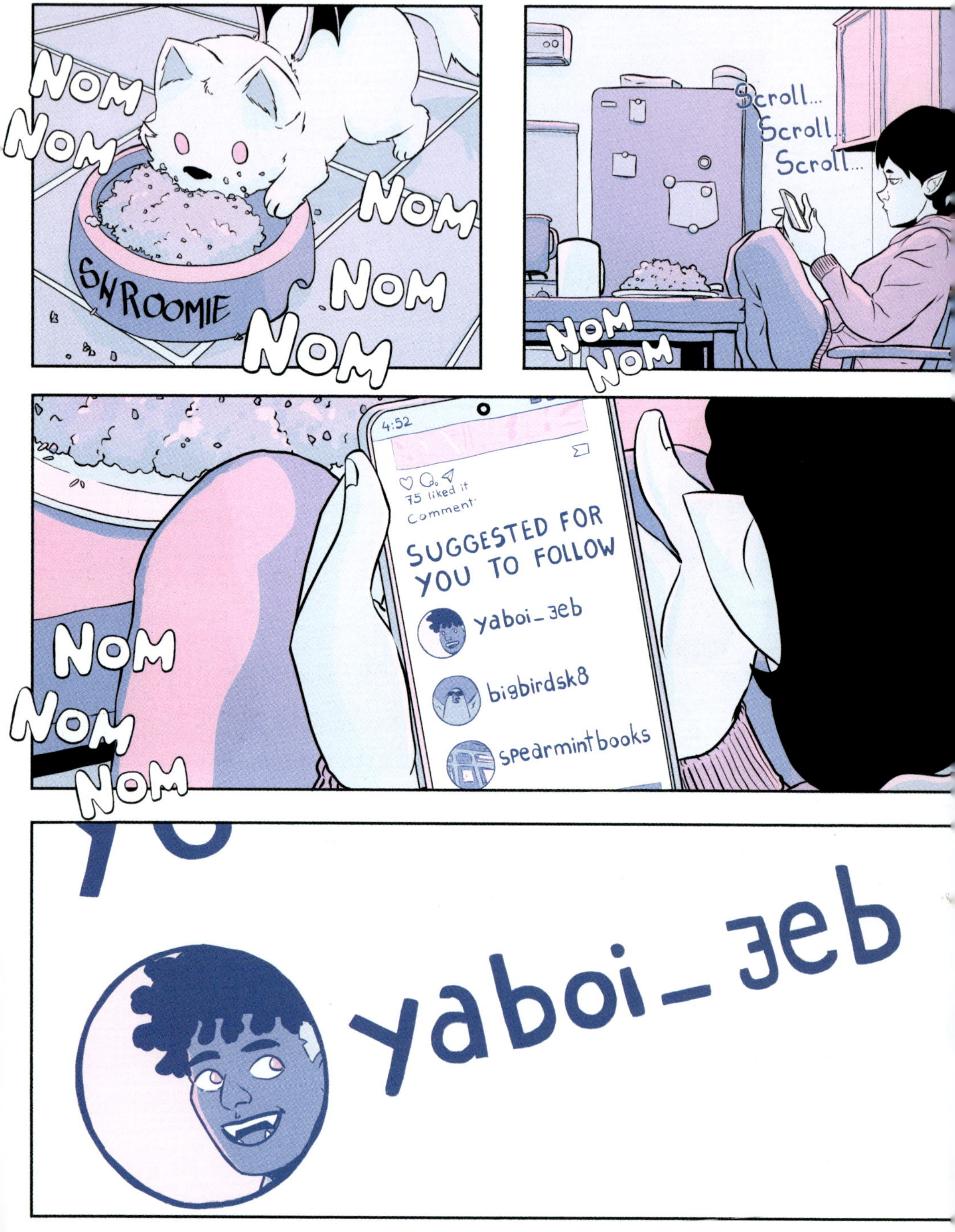

NOM
NOM
NOM
NOM
NOM
SHROOMIE

Scroll...
Scroll...
Scroll...
NOM
NOM

4:52
75 liked it
Comment
SUGGESTED FOR YOU TO FOLLOW
yaboi_ɜeb
bigbirdsk8
spearmintbooks
NOM
NOM
NOM

Scroll...
Click!

BURP!

YIP!
YIP!
YIP!
YIP!
YIP!
YIP!

YIP!
YIP!
YIP!
YIP!
YIP!
YIP!
YIP!
ALL RIGHT, **ALL RIGHT!** CAN I PUT ON SOME **SHOES** AT LEAST?

THAK

DANG, BRO!
AYYY!
WOO!

HAHA! CHEERS, GUYS!

KAW! KAW!!

SHROOM! STOP MENACING THE CROWS! THEY **DON'T** WANT TO BE YOUR FRIENDS!

EHH...

IT'S YOU!

YOU ARE THE SKATER LADY! I RECOGNIZED YOUR WINGS!

UMM, HEY! DO I **KNOW** YOU?
I SAW YOU DO A **REALLY COOL** TRICK ONCE! AT THE **BIG STAIRS!**

OH YEAH! WHEN WE DID THE **PHOTO SHOOT!** I REMEMBER!
R-REALLY? I...I...

I THOUGHT YOU WERE **SO COOL!** I TOLD MY MOM I WANT TO HAVE WINGS LIKE YOURS, BUT SHE SAID I'M TOO YOUNG TO BE A VAMPIRE, AND, LIKE, ONLY **LADY VAMPIRES** CAN HAVE WINGS, SO THAT'S SOMETHING I NEED TO THINK AB--

Y-YEAH. THAT'S TRUE. BUT, YOU KNOW, THE TRICK I DID THEN? OVER THE STAIRS?
YOU CAN TOTALLY DO THAT **WITHOUT** THE WINGS, JUST MAYBE OVER A SLIGHTLY SMALLER SET OF STEPS.
THE HARD PART IS THE **ACTUAL** SKATEBOARDING, **NOT** THE WINGS.

I KNOW, THAT'S WHY I'M LEARNING TO SKATE NOW, BUT I STILL WISH I COUL--
OH WOW! IS THAT A VAMPIRE DOG? WITH WINGS?
OH YES! THIS IS MY DOG, SHROOM!
DANG! BEING A VAMPIRE MUST BE **SO COOL!**
SKRITCH! SKRITCH!
ERR, I'M GONNA BE **LATE** FOR ORK, DAMN IT!
BLEET! BLEET!
SORRY, PAL, **GOTTA RUN!** KEEP ON PRACTICING OKAY?
I **WILL!**

THE LARK
THE LARK
DRINKS & FOOD
THE LARK PUB & RESTAURANT

YOU ARE LATE!
AGAIN!

ONLY BY FIVE MINUTES.
AND I'LL STAY ON AFTER WE CLOSE, TO HELP CLEAN UP!

YOU ALWAYS STAY ON!
THAT'S 'CAUSE I LIVE FOR THIS PLACE!
HAHH! THAT'S A GOOD ONE!
ALL RIGHT, GET ON WITH IT...

THE FOOD IS GETTING COLD!
THAT **MIGHT** IMPROVE IT.

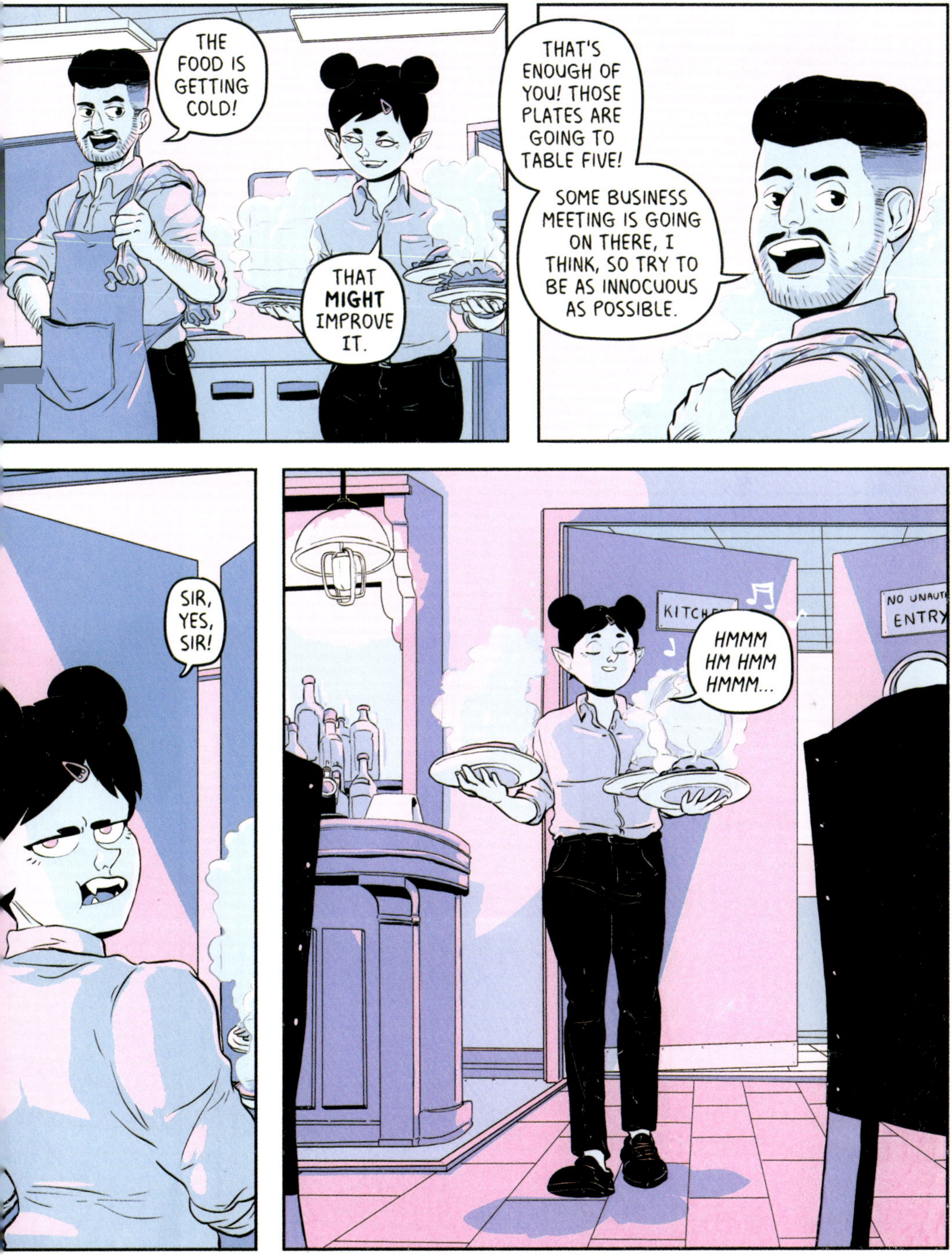

THAT'S ENOUGH OF YOU! THOSE PLATES ARE GOING TO TABLE FIVE!
SOME BUSINESS MEETING IS GOING ON THERE, I THINK, SO TRY TO BE AS INNOCUOUS AS POSSIBLE.

SIR, YES, SIR!

HMMM HM HMMM HMMM...

HEY, GUYS, I'M PEPPER, I WILL BE YOUR WAITRESS FROM NOW ON, SO JUST GIVE ME A SHOUT IF YOU NEED ANYTHING!

FIRST UP I GOT SOME STEAK AND BEANS HERE...
THAT'S GONNA BE ME!

TRIPLE CHEESE-BURGER FOR THE GENTLEMAN.

AND THEN...

HEY!
KLANK!

BAMM!
WHAT THE HECK?

I NEED TO LEAVE! NOW!

WHAT? YOU'VE JUST STARTED, LIKE, TWO MINUTES AGO!
OH GODS, I'M GONNA BE SICK!
WHERE IS THE BIN?
FOOD
PLASTIC

I DON'T KNOW WHAT'S GOTTEN INTO YOU, BUT YOU NEED TO--

BLEURG

SORRY, GUYS, I JUST NEED A FEW MINUTES!

HI, EVERYONE, I'M THE OWNER OF THE PLACE.
APOLOGIES FOR THE INCONVENIENCE!

OUR WAITER WAS **SUDDENLY** NOT FEELING WELL, AND HAD TO LEAVE FOR THE DAY.
I WILL BE **PERSONALLY** ATTENDING TO YOU FROM NOW ON, AND THE NEXT ROUND OF DRINKS IS ON THE **HOUSE,** TO MAKE UP FOR THIS LITTLE ACCIDENT.

IS SHE STILL **AROUND?** SHE IS A FRIEND OF MINE, AND I WANT TO MAKE SURE SHE IS OKAY!
SHE LEFT ABOUT A MINUTE AGO, BUT YOU MIGHT STILL BE ABLE TO CATCH HER IF YOU HURRY!

'SCUSE ME!

THE LARK
THE LARK
DRINKS & FOOD
TAXI

BB

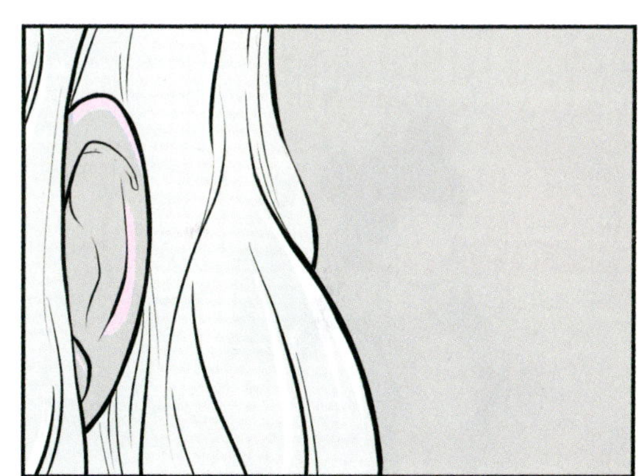

SHE'S...

SHE'S NOT...

SHE'S NOT A VAMP--

AAAAGH!

SKIFF

WOOAH!

PEPPER!

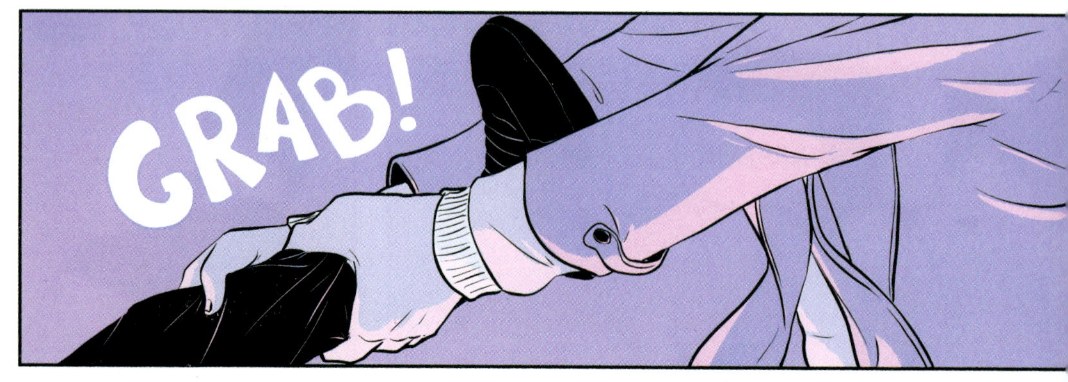
GRAB!

I GOT Y--

AAAAAH!

AAAAAH!

AAAAAH!

FWOOM!!

YOU...

YOU COULD HAVE DIED!
ARE YOU CRAZY?
WHAT? I TRIED TO SAVE YOU!
I GOT WINGS! YOU'VE SEEN ME FLY BEFORE!
THAT'S ACTUALLY A GOOD POINT. I DIDN'T THINK OF THAT IN THE MOMENT.
OH MY GODS, I ALMOST DIED!

HEY! HEY! THAT'S OKAY! I **GOT** YOU!
WHAT WERE YOU DOING UP THERE ANYWAY?
I COME UP HERE EVERY ONCE IN A WHILE TO CLEAR MY HEAD.

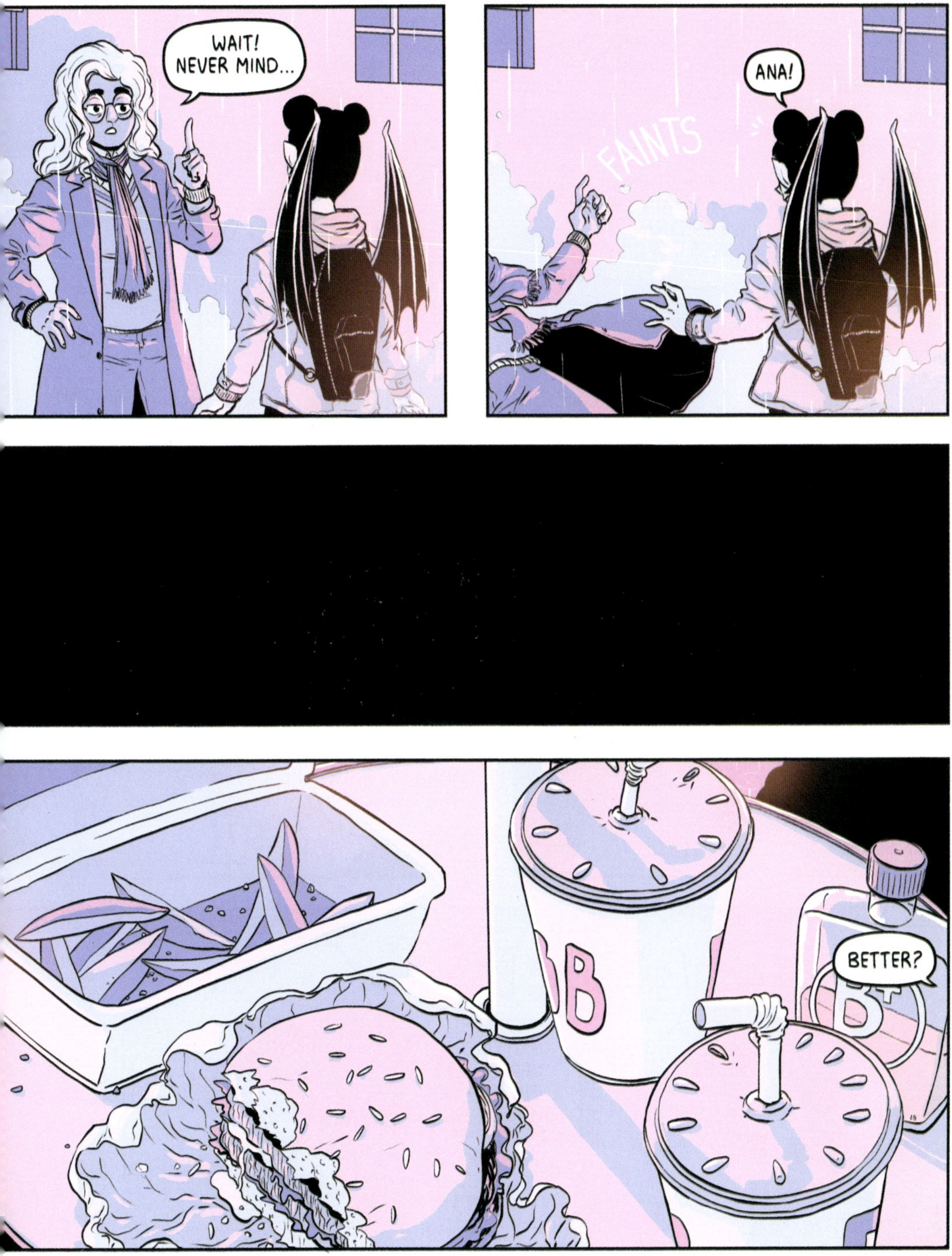

BETTER?

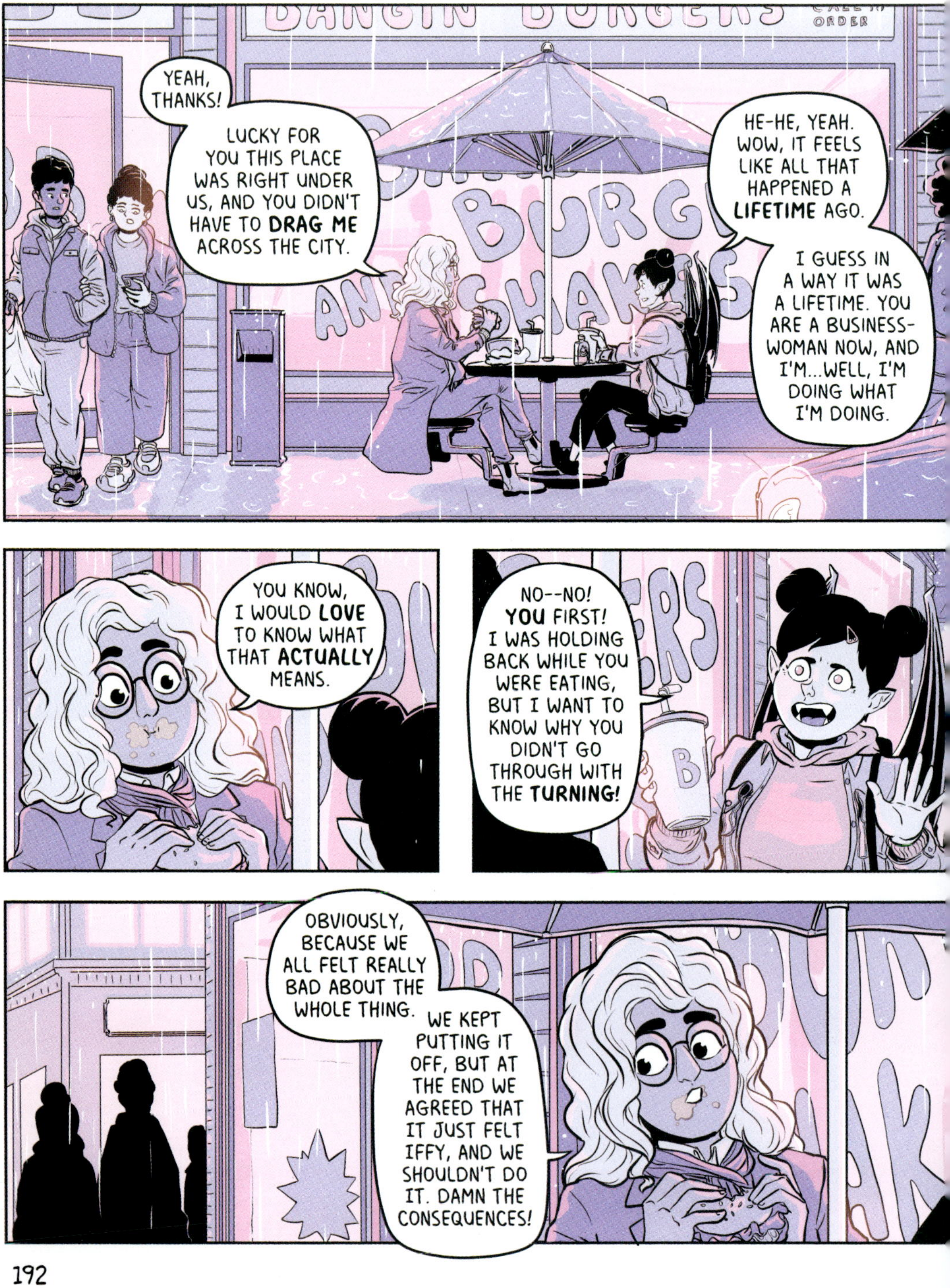

YEAH, THANKS!
LUCKY FOR YOU THIS PLACE WAS RIGHT UNDER US, AND YOU DIDN'T HAVE TO **DRAG ME** ACROSS THE CITY.
HE-HE, YEAH. WOW, IT FEELS LIKE ALL THAT HAPPENED A **LIFETIME** AGO.
I GUESS IN A WAY IT WAS A LIFETIME. YOU ARE A BUSINESS-WOMAN NOW, AND I'M...WELL, I'M DOING WHAT I'M DOING.

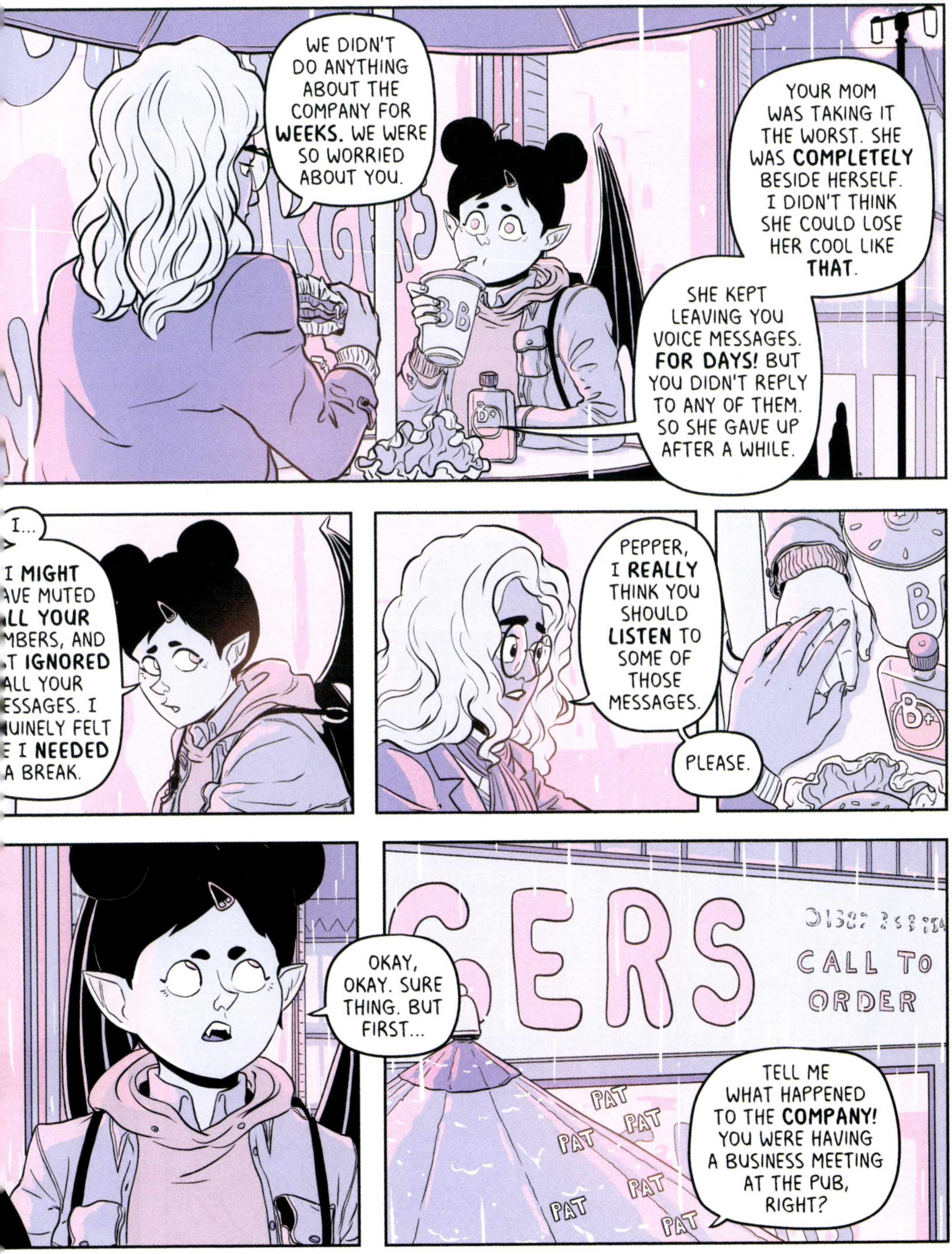

WE DIDN'T DO ANYTHING ABOUT THE COMPANY FOR **WEEKS.** WE WERE SO WORRIED ABOUT YOU.

YOUR MOM WAS TAKING IT THE WORST. SHE WAS **COMPLETELY** BESIDE HERSELF. I DIDN'T THINK SHE COULD LOSE HER COOL LIKE **THAT**.

SHE KEPT LEAVING YOU VOICE MESSAGES. **FOR DAYS!** BUT YOU DIDN'T REPLY TO ANY OF THEM. SO SHE GAVE UP AFTER A WHILE.

I WAS, YES. BITE IS ALIVE AND WELL. I THOUGHT YOU WOULD AT LEAST KEEP TABS ON THAT THROUGH OUR SOCIAL MEDIA OR SOMETHING.
I TRIED TO FOCUS ON MYSELF.

WHICH IS FAIR, BUT NOW I NEED TO QUICKLY CATCH YOU UP ON WHAT HAPPENED, AND...
WELL...

OKAY, SO, YOU KNOW WE NEEDED A PROPER VAMPIRE ON BOARD TO GET THE FUNDING FOR THE LAUNCH OF BITE, BUT WE BOTH BACKED OUT OF GETTING TURNED.
bite
WE WERE SO DOWN THAT WE JUST KIND OF DECIDED TO LET THE WHOLE THING FALL TO THE WAYSIDE.

ANIMAL RESCUE AND WELFARE
JEB WANTED A DISTRACTION, AND HE WAS REALLY MISSING SHROOM, SO, BELIEVE IT OR NOT, HE WENT TO VOLUNTEER AT AN ANIMAL SHELTER.

WHAT?

FIRST I THOUGHT HE ST WANTED TO **AST** ON SOME F THE MORE NFORTUNATE NIMALS WHO IDN'T QUITE RECOVER.
RUSTY

BUT TURNS OUT I MISJUDGED YOUR BROTHER AGAIN, BECAUSE HE PROVED TO BE A REAL ASSET TO THE PLACE.
EVEN WITHOUT ANY FINANCIAL GAINS, HE **REALLY** PUT HIS BACK INTO IT.

THEN ONE NIGHT, A RANDOM GUY BROUGHT IN A DOG HE'D FOUND AT THE SIDE OF THE ROAD.

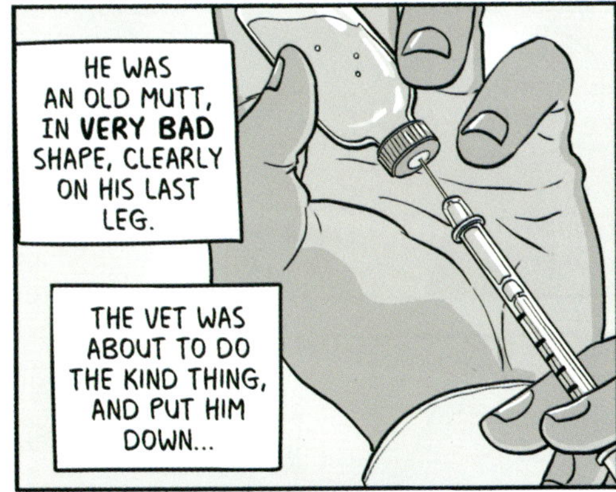
HE WAS AN OLD MUTT, IN **VERY BAD** SHAPE, CLEARLY ON HIS LAST LEG.
THE VET WAS ABOUT TO DO THE KIND THING, AND PUT HIM DOWN...

WHEN JEB STEPPED IN.
APPARENTLY, IT WAS THE FIRST DOG HE EVER SAW DYING IN FRONT OF HIM, AND HE JUST COULDN'T TAKE IT.

AND I **FULLY** BELIEVE HE DID WHAT HE DID BECAUSE HE WANTED TO **SAVE** THE POOR FELLA.

WAIT!
WHAT?

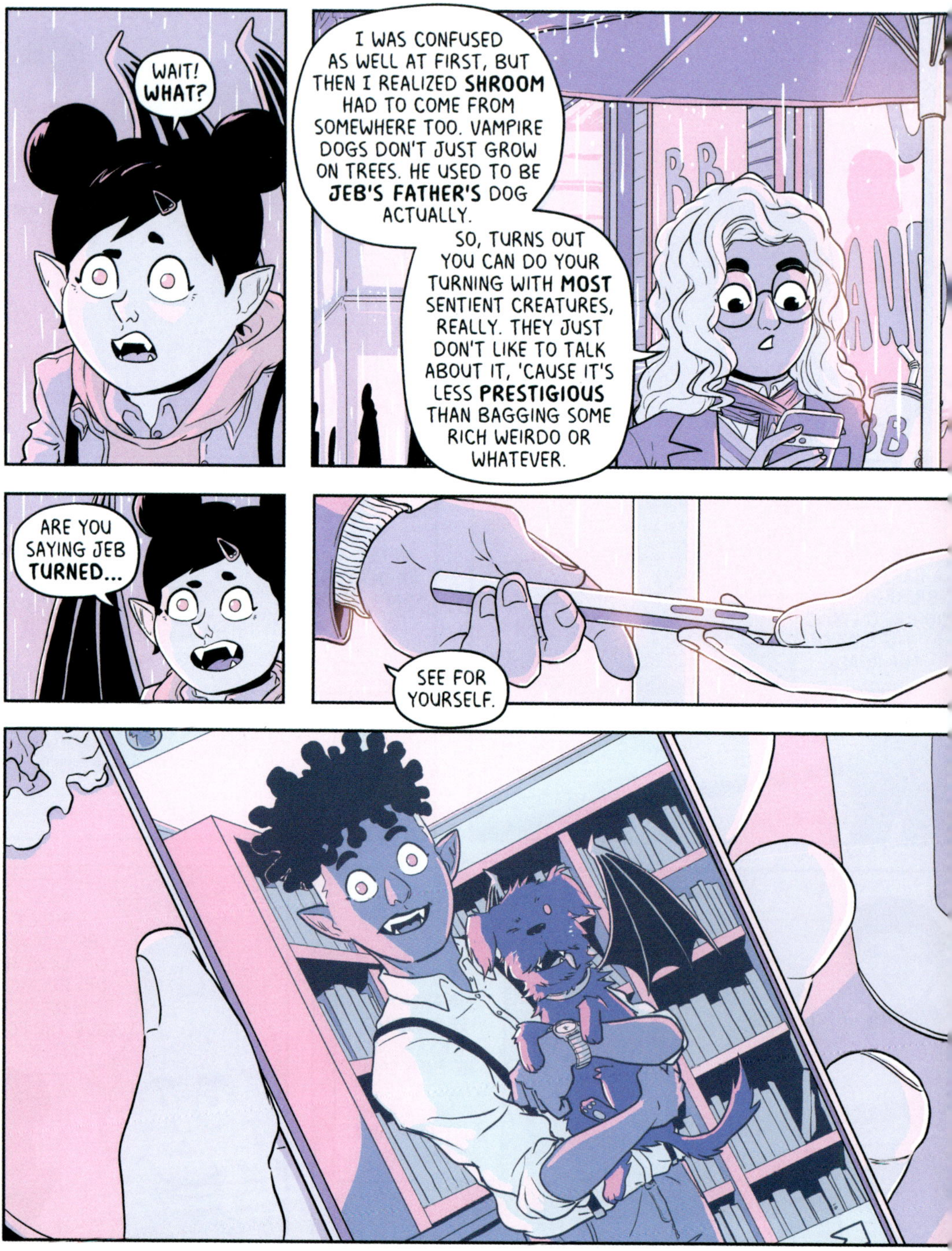

I WAS CONFUSED AS WELL AT FIRST, BUT THEN I REALIZED **SHROOM** HAD TO COME FROM SOMEWHERE TOO. VAMPIRE DOGS DON'T JUST GROW ON TREES. HE USED TO BE **JEB'S FATHER'S** DOG ACTUALLY.
SO, TURNS OUT YOU CAN DO YOUR TURNING WITH **MOST** SENTIENT CREATURES, REALLY. THEY JUST DON'T LIKE TO TALK ABOUT IT, 'CAUSE IT'S LESS **PRESTIGIOUS** THAN BAGGING SOME RICH WEIRDO OR WHATEVER.

ARE YOU SAYING JEB **TURNED...**

SEE FOR YOURSELF.

YOUR BROTHER BECAME A **PROPER** VAMPIRE BY **TURNING** A DOG, JUST LIKE HIS **FATHER** DID.
AND WITH THAT DONE, WE MANAGED TO SECURE THE FUNDING FOR **BITE**.

HE BECAME A BIT OF A LAUGHINGSTOCK IN VAMPIRE CIRCLES BECAUSE HE TURNED A DOG, BUT THAT ACTUALLY HELPED WITH PROMOTING OUR LAUNCH AS WELL.

I... HONESTLY, I **DID NOT** SEE THAT COMING.
SOMETIMES PEOPLE CAN SURPRISE YOU.

SO... WHAT DO YOU THINK?

MAYBE IT'S TIME TO LISTEN TO SOME OF YOUR MOM'S MESSAGES?

SPEAR MINT CONDITION
ANTIQUE & SECOND

I THINK THAT'S IT FOR TONIGHT. THANKS FOR HELPING OUT, HONEY.

ANYTIME! **MOSS** LOVES TO HANG OUT IN THE SHOP TOO.
RIGHT, BOY?

MMR?

DING
DEENG
AH, SORRY, BUT WE ARE CLOSED FOR TO--

JEB, YOU LITTLE MISCREANT!

STOMP!
STOMP!
STOMP!

DID YOU TURN A SICK, OLD DOG INTO YOUR FOREVER COMPANION?

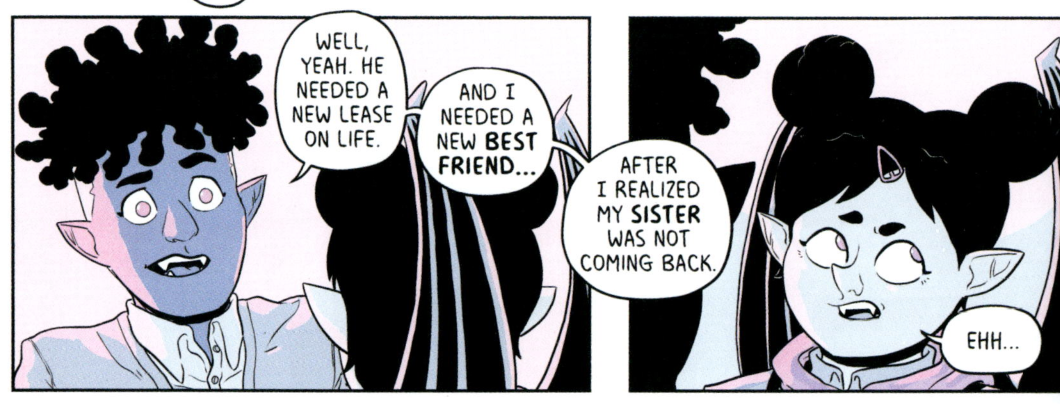
WELL, YEAH. HE NEEDED A NEW LEASE ON LIFE.
AND I NEEDED A NEW BEST FRIEND...
AFTER I REALIZED MY SISTER WAS NOT COMING BACK.
EHH...

ARE YOU ANGRY?
ANGRY? NAH, I JUST WANTED TO SCARE YOU A BIT.

HOW CAN ANYONE BE ANGRY AT THIS?

YEAH, SO THAT'S MOSS. FEEL FREE TO PET HIM. HE'S CHILL.
I'M GLAD TO SEE YOU AGAIN, BUT I ASSUME YOU DIDN'T JUST REAPPEAR AFTER MONTHS TO PET MY DOG?
NOT GONNA LIE, HE **WAS** A BIG FACTOR, BUT I ALSO CAME TO SMOOTH THINGS OUT A BIT.
I LEFT YOU GUYS WITHOUT CONSIDERING THE RAMIFICATIONS FOR YOU.

BELIEVE IT OR NOT, BUSINESS WAS **THE LEAST** OF MY WORRIES.
THOUGHT IT WOULD BE YOURS, TOO. ALWAYS FELT LIKE IT WAS SOMETHING I WAS PUSHING ON YOU AGAINST YOUR WILL.

A BIT, YEAH...
BUT MAYBE I **NEEDED** THAT PUSH TO TRY SOMETHING I WOULDN'T HAVE OTHERWISE.

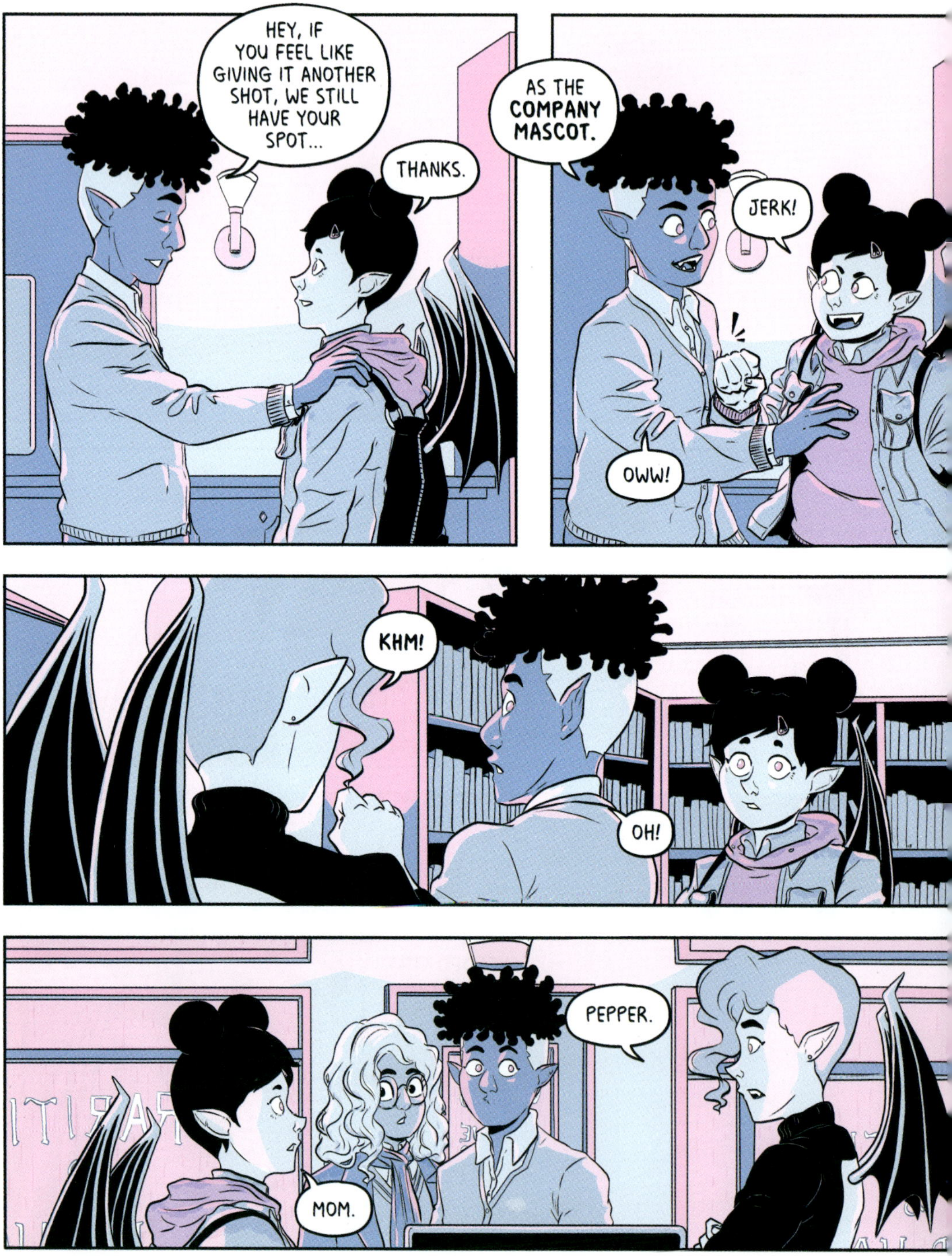

HEY, IF YOU FEEL LIKE GIVING IT ANOTHER SHOT, WE STILL HAVE YOUR SPOT...
THANKS.
AS THE **COMPANY MASCOT.**
JERK!
OWW!

SHOULD I BE **WORRIED?**

SO, I... LEFT YOU A **COUPLE** OF MESSAGES...

FIFTY-SEVEN, TO BE PRECISE.

THAT MANY, HUH?
DID... DID YOU HAVE TIME TO LISTEN TO **ANY** OF THEM?

YEAH, I... SKIMMED THROUGH SOME...
ABOUT FORTY-FIVE MINUTES AGO.
PAT
PAT
PAT
PAT
PAT
PAT
PEPPER...? IT'S MOM AGAIN.
I DON'T KNOW IF YOU BLOCKED ME OR JUST DECIDED NOT TO LISTEN TO MY MESSAGES, BUT I HOPE IF YOU WILL EVENTUALLY LISTEN TO ONE, IT WILL BE THIS ONE.
I JUST... I JUST WANT TO SAY I'M SORRY.
I'M JUST SORRY FOR HOW OUR RELATIONSHIP DEVELOPED.
GAH! I SOUND SO COLD AND CLINICAL AGAIN!
Hic!
THAT'S JUST HOW I AM, I GUESS. BUT PLEASE KNOW THAT ALL I EVER WANTED IS FOR YOU TO BE HAPPY, BECAUSE I LOVE YOU SO, SO VERY MUCH!

AND I KNOW THAT'S NOT AN EXCUSE!
SNIF!
I PUSHED YOU TOO HARD AND DIDN'T CONSIDER THAT WHAT WAS RIGHT FOR ME MIGHT NOT BE RIGHT FOR YOU.
Hic!
AND I KNOW THAT NOW, WHEN IT MIGHT BE TOO LATE, BECAUSE I FINALLY PUSHED YOU TOO MUCH!
I HOPE YOU KNOW THAT YOU CAN COME HOME WHENEVER YOU FEEL LIKE.
SOB!
SOB!
I JUST...I DON'T CARE ABOUT YOUR TURNING OR ANYTHING ELSE. I JUST DON'T WANT YOU TO BE ALONE AND ON YOUR OWN!
RGERS
CALL TO ORDER
SOB!
THAT'S MY WORST FEAR.

PEPPER?
SNIFF!
I THINK... I THINK I JUST HAVE AN **ALLERGIC REACTION** TO THE MILKSHAKE.

MHMM...
DO YOU THINK **A HUG** WOULD HELP?
SNORT!
I'M **REALLY** SNOTTY.
IT'S OKAY. I FEEL LIKE I'M ABOUT TO GET **REALLY SNOTTY** TOO.

SNIF!
THEN... CAN I GET A HUG, PLEASE?

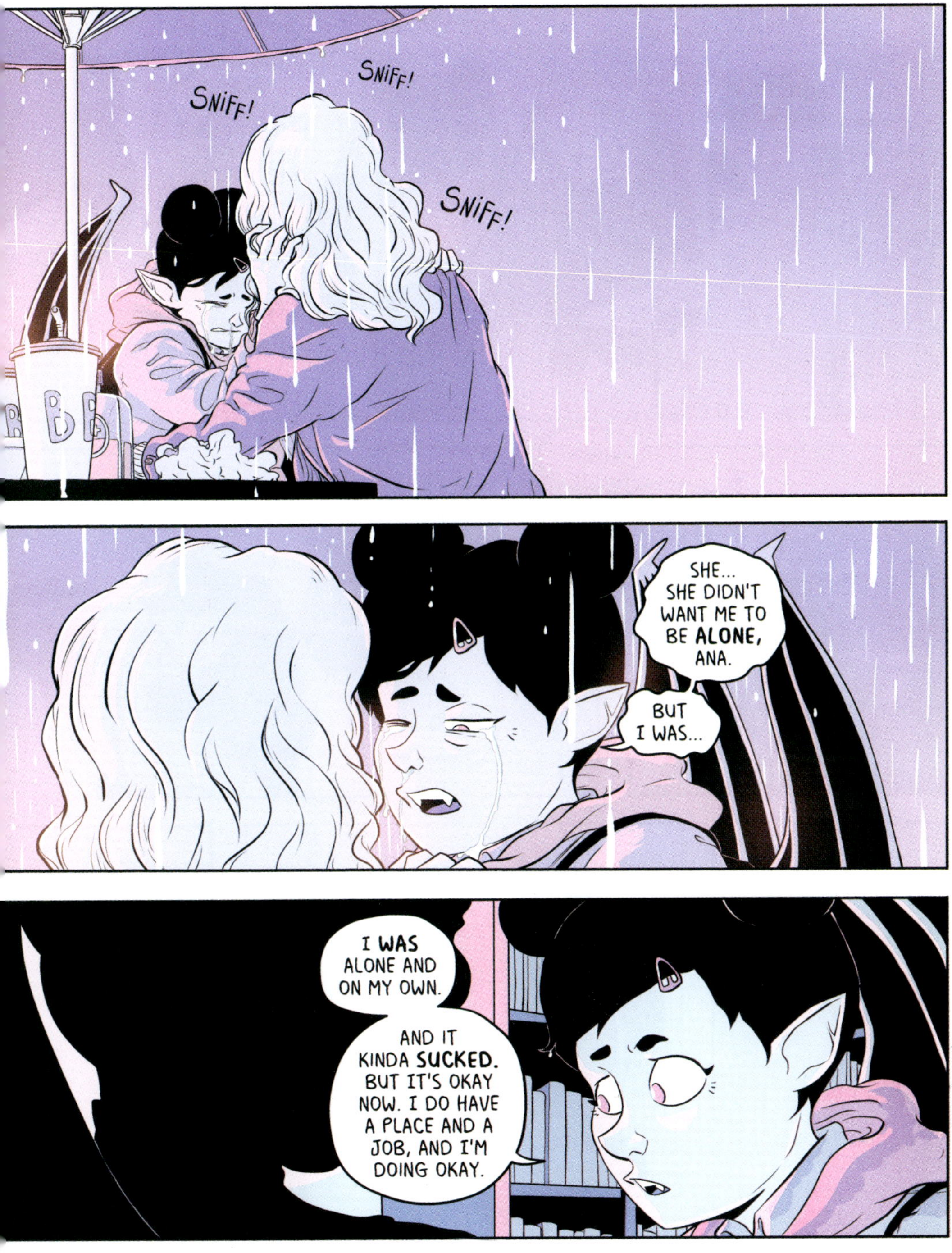

SNIFF!
SNIFF!
SNIFF!

BUT **MAYBE** I SHOULDN'T HAVE CUT OFF SO DRASTICALLY...
PART OF WHAT MADE ME **ME**.

HONEY...
YOU ARE **ALWAYS** GOING TO BE **YOU**.

I LEARNED THAT THE **HARD WAY**.

KRKK!

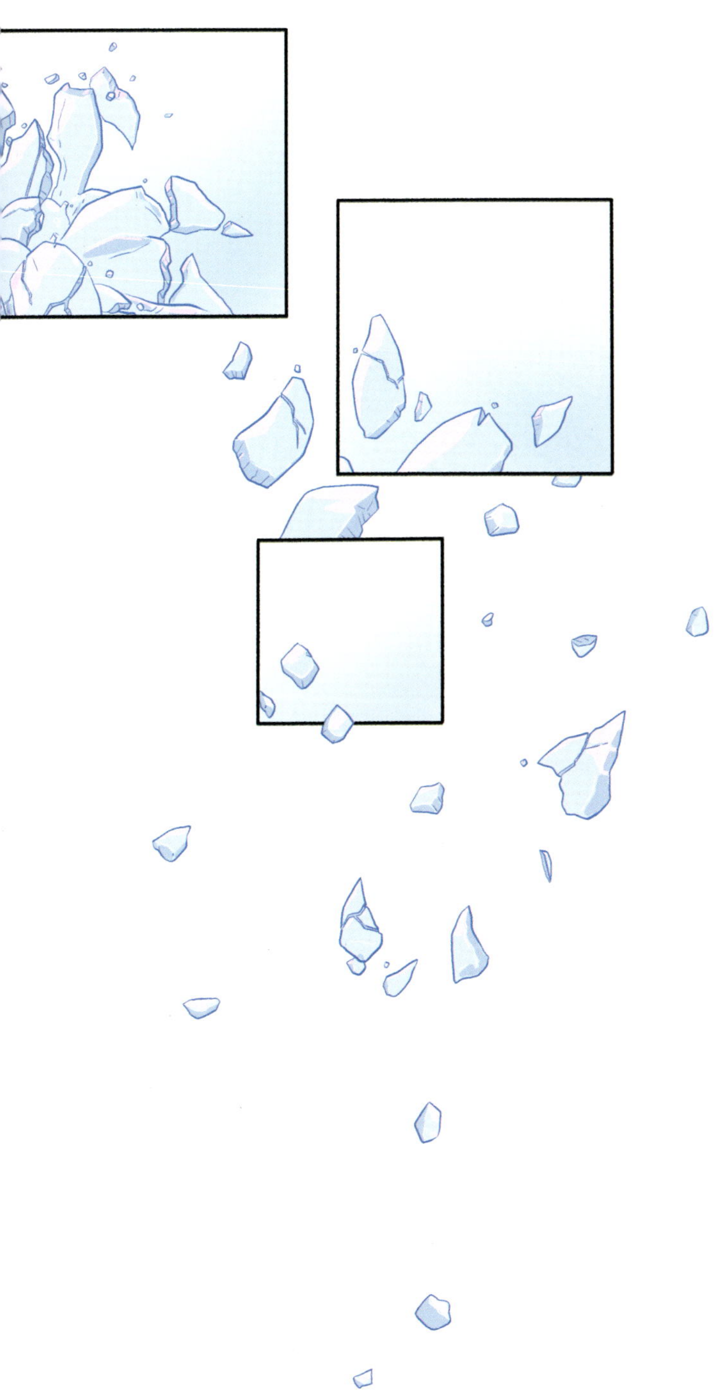

SPEARMINT CONDITION
DING DEENG
USED

SED
&
ANTIQUE
Rustle
Rustle

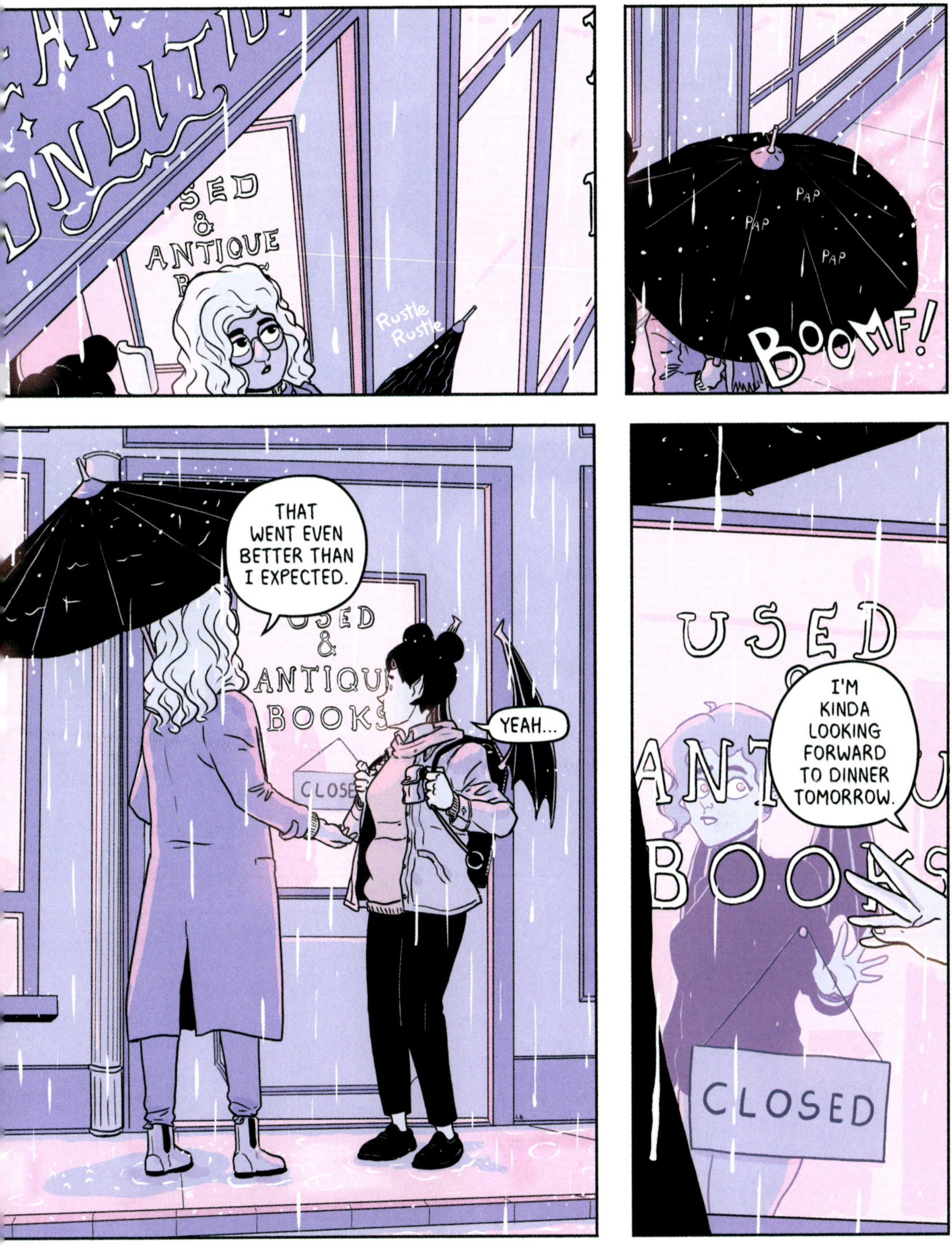

PAP
PAP
PAP
BOOMF!

THAT WENT EVEN BETTER THAN I EXPECTED.
YEAH...

USED
I'M KINDA LOOKING FORWARD TO DINNER TOMORROW.
CLOSED

I'M LOOKING FORWARD TO IT TOO!
MAKE SURE TO BRING **SHROOM** WITH YOU AS WELL.

OH MY **GODS!**
I **COMPLETELY** FORGOT I LEFT HIM ALONE **ALL DAY!**
HE PROBABLY DEMOLISHED THE **WHOLE** APARTMENT BY NOW!

AH, WELL! IF YOUR LANDLORD THROWS YOU OUT, I'M SURE YOU WILL FIND A NEW PLACE IN NO TIME.
OR YOU CAN CRASH ON THE COUCH IN THE LIVING ROOM, 'CAUSE I KINDA TOOK OVER YOUR ROOM.

YOUR BED IS PRETTY COMFY.

CONDITION
KIDDING! WANT ME TO WALK YOU HOME AND HELP CLEAN UP?
I WOULD LOVE TO SEE SHROOM AGAIN AS WELL.
ANTIQUE & SECOND HAND BOOKS

SPEAR MINT CONDITION
USED & ANTIQUE BOOKS
CLOSED
RARITIES & PECULIARS
HAHA! THANKS, I WAS SO CONFUSED FOR A SECOND.
GOOD! THAT MEANS I STILL GOT IT!
WHAT?
YOU.

SUMMER
AGAIN.

VIDS
HEY, FOLKS! IT'S ME, JEB, GETTING READY FOR THE NEXT **BITE** PHOTO SHOOT!
bite_sk8
Live now!
comment
VIDS
IT FEELS ALMOST NOSTALGIC REVISITING THESE STEPS AGAIN AFTER A YEAR. BUT THIS IS WHERE WE DID OUR **VERY FIRST** PHOTO SHOOT, BELIEVE IT OR NOT!
SO, WE THOUGHT WE SHOULD CELEBRATE **BITE'S** ANNIVERSARY BY DRAGGING **PEPPER** OUT HERE, AND MAKING HER DO AN **EVEN CRAZIER** TRICK THAN LAST TIME!
SHE IS READY!
bite_sk8
Live now!
comment

VIDS
ALL RIGHT, GUYS! DON'T FORGET TO **LIKE AND SUBSCRIBE.** AND IF YOU ARE A YOUNG **VAMPIRE,** WANTING TO GET OUT THERE AND TRY OUT SOME ATHLETICS, JUST LIKE OUR PEPPER, THEN CHECK OUT OUR SPONSOR: B+ SPORTS JUICE!
bite_sk8
live now!
comment
JEB!
OKAY, **HERE SHE COMES!**
bite_sk8
live now!

VIDS

bite_sk8

Live now!

comment...

PAKK!

FWOOM!

END.

TO ALL THE PEOPLE WHO HELPED ME
MAKE PEPPER WHO SHE BECAME:
DANIELLA, TAMAS, AND JEAN; MY AGENT, BRENT;
AND THE LOVELY PEOPLE AT MCELDERRY BOOKS,
KATE, MICHAEL, AND ANDRENAE.
AND TO YOU FOR READING.

MARGARET K. MCELDERRY BOOKS
AN IMPRINT OF SIMON & SCHUSTER CHILDREN'S PUBLISHING DIVISION
1230 AVENUE OF THE AMERICAS, NEW YORK, NEW YORK 10020

FOR INFORMATION ABOUT SPECIAL DISCOUNTS FOR BULK PURCHASES, PLEASE CONTACT SIMON & SCHUSTER SPECIAL SALES AT 1-866-506-1949 OR BUSINESS@SIMONANDSCHUSTER.COM.
THE SIMON & SCHUSTER SPEAKERS BUREAU CAN BRING AUTHORS TO YOUR LIVE EVENT. FOR MORE INFORMATION OR TO BOOK AN EVENT, CONTACT THE SIMON & SCHUSTER SPEAKERS BUREAU AT 1-866-248-3049 OR VISIT OUR WEBSITE AT WWW.SIMONSPEAKERS.COM.
THE TEXT FOR THIS BOOK WAS SET IN MILK MUSTACHE BB.
THE ILLUSTRATIONS FOR THIS BOOK WERE RENDERED DIGITALLY.
MANUFACTURED IN CHINA
FIRST EDITION
2 4 6 8 10 9 7 5 3 1
CIP DATA FOR THIS BOOK IS AVAILABLE FROM THE LIBRARY OF CONGRESS.
ISBN 9781665970471 (HC)
ISBN 9781665970464 (PBK)
ISBN 9781665970488 (EBOOK)